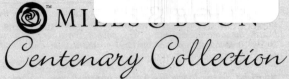

**Celebrating 100 years of romance with
the very best of Mills & Boon**

*First published in Great Britain 2008
by Harlequin Mills & Boon Limited,
Eton House, 18-24 Paradise Road, Richmond, Surrey TW9 1SR*

© Lucy Gordon 2001

ISBN: 978 0 263 86647 6

76-1208

*Harlequin Mills & Boon policy is to use papers that are
natural, renewable and recyclable products and made from
wood grown in sustainable forests. The logging and
manufacturing processes conform to the legal environmental
regulations of the country of origin.*

*Printed and bound in Spain
by Litografia Rosés S.A., Barcelona*

Christmas in Venice

by
Lucy Gordon

MILLS & BOON

Pure reading pleasure

Lucy Gordon cut her writing teeth on magazine journalism, interviewing many of the world's most interesting men, including Warren Beatty, Richard Chamberlain, Sir Roger Moore, Sir Alec Guinness, and Sir John Gielgud. She also camped out with lions in Africa and had many other unusual experiences which have often provided the background for her books. She is married to a Venetian, whom she met while on holiday in Venice. They got engaged within two days.

Two of her books have won the Romance Writers of America RITA® award, *Song of the Lorelei* in 1990, and *His Brother's Child* in 1998 in the Best Traditional Romance category.

You can visit her website at www.lucy-gordon.com

CHAPTER ONE

JUST a few more minutes—just ten—then five—
then they would reach Venice, the city Sonia had
sworn never to set foot in again. As the train rumbled
across the lagoon she refused to look out of the
window. She knew what she would see if she did.
First, the blue water, sparkling under the winter sun,
then the roofs and gilded cupolas, gradually
emerging from the mist on the horizon. It was
perfect, magical, a sight to lift the heart. And she
didn't want to see it.

Venice, the loveliest place in Italy, in the world.
She'd come here once before, and later fled,
blaming it for her misfortunes. But for the summer
beauty of the city she might never have been
tempted into a disastrous marriage to Francesco
Bartini. She knew better now. She'd fled Francesco
and the heartbreakingly beautiful surroundings
where they'd met, vowing never to be seduced by
either of them again.

She tried not to think of him as he had seemed to her then, smiling, at ease with himself and everyone around him. He wasn't handsome—his features weren't regular enough for that, his nose too large, his mouth too wide. But his eyes were dark and full of delicious wickedness, his smile was brilliant, and when he laughed he was irresistible. She'd been enchanted by his charm and good nature, the speed with which he'd fallen in love with her, as though he'd been only waiting for her to appear to recognise the love of his life.

'But that's true,' he'd said once. 'Why delay when you've met "the one"?'

He'd been so sure she was 'the one' that he'd made her believe it too. But Venice had helped him, with its beauty, its glitter of romance that was there around every corner. Venice had helped to deceive her into thinking a holiday flirtation was a lasting love, and she would never forgive Venice for that.

So why was she coming back?

Because Tomaso, her father-in-law, had begged her, and she had always liked him. Even in the bad days of her marriage the hot-tempered little man had always made her feel how fond of her he was. On the day she left he had wept, 'Please, Sonia—don't go—I beg you—*ti prego*—'

Officially, she was only returning to England for a visit, to 'see how she felt'. But none of them were fooled, especially Tomaso. He knew she wasn't coming back.

He'd held onto her, weeping openly, and his wife, Giovanna, had regarded him with scorn, because who cared if the stupid English wife left? She'd been a mistake from the start and thank goodness Francesco had realised at last.

Tomaso had wept despite his wife, and Sonia had wept with him. But still she had left. She'd had to. But now she was back, because Tomaso had begged her.

'Giovanna is very ill,' he'd said, the day he turned up at her London apartment. 'She knows she treated you badly, and it weighs on her. Come home and let her make her peace with you.'

'Not home, *Poppa*. It was never a home to me.'

'But we all loved you.'

And that was true, she reflected. With one exception they had all loved, or at least liked her: Francesco's sisters in-law, his three brothers, his aunts, his uncle, his endless cousins, had all smiled and welcomed her. Only Giovanna, his mother, had frowned and been suspicious.

How could she return? It was nearly Christmas. Travelling would be a nightmare. Worse, she would have to see Francesco again, and what would they say to each other after the last dreadful meeting in London? He'd followed her there to make one final effort to save their marriage, and when it failed he'd been curt and bitter.

'I won't plead with you any more,' he'd raged. 'I thought I could convince you that our love was worth saving, but what do you know of love?'

'I know that ours was a mistake,' she'd cried, 'if it was love at all. Sometimes I think it wasn't—just a pretty illusion.'

He'd given a mirthless laugh directed at himself. 'How easily you talk love away when it suits you. The more fool me, for thinking you had a woman's heart. Well, you've convinced me. You want no more of me, and now I want no more of you. Go to hell in your own way, and I will go in mine.'

She'd never seen him like that before. In their short marriage he'd been angry many times, with the hot temper of the Latin, flaring now and forgotten a moment later. But this bitter, decided rejection was different. She should have been glad that he'd accepted her decision, but instead she was unaccountably desolate.

She'd tried to be sensible. She'd told herself that that was that, and she could draw a line under her marriage.

But the very next morning she'd woken up feeling queasy, and known that everything had changed. There had been tests but the result was never in doubt. She was carrying Francesco's child, and she'd learned it the day after he'd stormed out declaring he wanted no more of her.

She heard his voice many times repeating those

words. She heard it every time she reached for the phone to tell him about their baby, and it always made her pull her hand back, until at last she no longer tried.

So when Tomaso had arrived in London his eyes had opened wide at the sight that met him.

'You're having his child and he doesn't know?' he demanded, shocked.

It had touched her heart the way he never doubted the baby was Francesco's. But Tomaso had always thought the best of her, she recalled. It made it hard to refuse him, although she'd tried.

'How can I go back now?' she'd said, indicating her pregnancy. 'When Francesco sees me like this it will revive things that are best forgotten.'

'Don't worry,' Tomaso had reassured her. 'Francesco is courting someone else.'

She'd suppressed the little inner shock, the voice that cried out, 'So soon?' After all, she had left him. He was a warm-hearted man who wouldn't stay alone for long. She had no right to complain.

She insisted that Francesco must be warned before she arrived, and Tomaso telephoned his son and gabbled something in the Venetian dialect which Sonia had never been able to follow. When the call was over he'd announced, 'No problem. Francesco says the baby is yours. He won't interfere.'

'That's fine,' she'd said, trying to sound pleased.

Well, it *was* fine. It was exactly what she wanted. If he wasn't interested in his own baby that suited her perfectly. And if she was being unreasonable, so what? She was eight months pregnant and entitled to be unreasonable.

Because she was so close to her time they couldn't fly, and had embarked on the twenty-four-hour train journey. That was how she'd made her first trip, because she'd booked at the last minute and couldn't get a flight. So she'd approached Venice by train over the lagoon and seen it rising from the sea in glory.

Tomaso glanced at her as she sat, refusing to go to the window. 'After all this time, don't you want to see Venice welcoming you back?'

'Oh, *Poppa*, that's just a pretty fantasy,' Sonia protested, smiling to take the sting out of the words. 'Venice deals in pretty fantasies, and I made the mistake of taking them seriously.'

'And now you make the mistake of blaming the city for being beautiful,' he replied.

'So beautiful that I fell in love with it, and thought that was the same as being in love with a man.'

He was silent, but regarded her sadly.

'All right, I'll take a look,' she said to please him.

But the sight that met her wasn't what she had expected. Where was the magic, the gradual appearance of gilded cupolas touched by the sun? How could she have forgotten that this was late December? A dank mist lay on the sea, shrouding the little city so that there was no sign of it. When at last it crept into view—reluctantly, it seemed to Sonia—it had a glum, heavy-hearted appearance that reflected her own feelings.

At the station she tried to carry her own bags but Tomaso flew into a temper until she let him take them. He commandeered one of the taxi boats, and gave the driver the name of her hotel. The Cornucopia.

Of course, he didn't know that this was where she'd stayed that first time. No matter. She would enter the Cornucopia again and banish her ghosts.

She'd had to brace herself for the sight of the Grand Canal on leaving the station. The railway station had a broad flight of steps leading down to the water and, on the far side, the magnificent Church of San Simeone. It had made her catch her breath when she first saw it three years ago, and again when she had arrived there in a gondola to be married, a few short weeks later. Now she tried not to look, but to concentrate as Tomaso handed her carefully down into one of the taxi boats in this city where the streets were water.

The chugging of the motor boat made her a little queasy, so she didn't have to look at the palaces and hotels gliding past. But she was aware of them anyway, she knew them so well, and every tiny *rio* as each little side canal was called: Rio della Pergola, Rio della due Torri, Rio di Noale, taking her closer to the Cornucopia, until at last it came in sight.

The Cornucopia had once been the palace of a great Venetian nobleman, and the company that had turned it into an hotel had restored its glory. Beneath the mediaeval magnificence was a good deal of modern comfort, but discreet, so that the atmosphere might be undisturbed.

She was booked into a comfortable suite on the second floor.

'You look tired,' Tomaso told her. 'You need a rest after that journey. I'll leave you now, and call back in a few hours to take you to see Giovanna.'

He kissed her cheek and departed. It was a relief to be alone, to wash the journey off, and ease her heavy body onto the bed.

At least she wasn't in the same room as before. Then the city had been full for the Venice Glass Fair, with not a room to be had. Sonia, booking at the last minute, had been forced to accept a place nobody else wanted, at the top of the building.

It had been little more than an attic, she recalled, but she'd had her own bathroom, and she'd hurried into the shower to wash off the journey. When she'd finished she'd taken a whirl around the tiny room, thrilled by her first foreign trip for her employers, and her first visit to Venice. At this height there were only the birds to see her, and she finished by tossing aside her towel and standing, arms ecstatically upstretched in a shaft of sunlight from the window.

The door opened and a young man came in.

She was totally naked, her position emphasising her perfect body, long legs, tiny waist and full breasts. And he was barely six feet away with a grandstand view.

For what seemed like forever they stared at each other, neither able to move.

Then he blushed. Even now it could make her smile to think that he had been the one to blush.

'*Scusi, signorina, scusi, scusi…*' He backed out hastily and shut the door.

She stared at the panels, but all she saw was his face, mobile, vivid, fascinating, blotting out everything else in the world. Only then did she remember to be indignant.

'*Oi!*' she yelled, snatching up her towel and dashing for the door. In the corridor outside she found a pile of large boxes, two hefty workmen and the young man. 'What's the idea of barging into my room like that?'

'But it's *my* room,' the young man protested. 'At least, it was supposed to be—nobody told me you were here. If they had—' his eyes flickered over her and he seemed to be having difficulty breathing '—if they had, I—I would have been here twice as fast—'

Her lips twitched. Mad as she was, she wasn't immune to the flattery in those last words, or something in his look that went deeper than flattery.

The towel, inadequate at the best of times, was slipping badly. The two workmen watched her until the young man snapped something out and they vanished hurriedly.

'Let me put something on,' she said, retreating into her room, and grabbing a robe. The young man followed as if in a trance. She would have gone into the bathroom but she'd backed herself onto the wrong side of the bed.

'I don't look,' he said, understanding.

He turned away and covered his eyes in a theatrical fashion that made her laugh despite her agitation.

'No peeking,' he promised over his shoulder. 'I am a gentleman.'

'You shouldn't have followed me in here. That's not the act of a gentleman.'

'It's the act of a man,' he said with meaning.

She tied the belt firmly in place. 'OK, I'm decent now.'

He looked around. 'Yes, you are,' he agreed sadly.

'Will you please tell me what you're doing in my room?'

'Tomorrow the Venice Glass Fair starts, and one of the biggest exhibitions is in this hotel. The manager is a friend of mine. He said nobody ever wants this room, so I could use it to store some of my glass.'

'I booked at the last minute. I think it was the only room left in the city.'

'Forgive me, I should have checked.' He gave a rueful, winning smile. 'But then we would never have met. And that would have been a tragedy.'

There was a note in his voice that made her clutch the edges of the robe together lest he detect that her whole body was singing. Just a few words, and the glow in his eyes, and she felt as though he was touching her all over.

He had a slim, lithe figure and wonderful dark eyes, set in a lean, tanned face, still boyish as it probably always would be. Sonia was a tall woman but she had to look up to see his black hair with its touch of curl.

'You—you're exhibiting in the glass fair, then?' she said.

'That's right. I own a small factory, and I'm here to set up my stall.'

'I'm here for the fair. I'm a glass buyer for a store in England.'

His face lit up. 'Then you must let me take you on a tour of my factory. It's here.' He took a card from his pocket. 'Only a few tours for specially privileged visitors—'

'Would you mind if I got dressed first?'

'Of course. Forgive me. Besides I have to find somewhere for my glass.'

'But won't you have it downstairs on the stall?'

'Some yes, but some will be sold, or given away, or broken. So I must have spares nearby.'

'Doesn't the hotel provide you with storage space?'

'Of course, but—I've brought rather more than I should. I thought I could make it all right.'

Later she was to discover that this was his way: bend the rules and worry about the practical problems afterwards. And it usually did work out, because he had such charm and confidence. Even then, ten minutes after their meeting, Sonia found herself saying, 'Look, I don't mind—if there isn't too much.'

'There is nothing—almost nothing—you'll never notice it.'

In fact there were ten large boxes, but she didn't see the danger until they were all crowded into her room so that she could barely move. And then she lacked the heart to tell him to take them away. She'd even helped him carry them in. She'd actually *offered*. He was like that.

'Never mind,' she said brightly. 'There won't be so much when you've set up your stall.'

'It's up,' he explained. 'This is just the extras. You really are a bit cramped, aren't you?'

She gave him a baleful look.

'There's nothing for it,' he said with a sigh. 'I shall have to take you out to dinner.'

'That will be impossible,' she said crossly.

'Why?'

'Because all my clothes are in the wardrobe that is now completely blocked by your boxes.'

It took them ten minutes to get the wardrobe door clear, and then he wouldn't let her choose her dress in peace.

'Not that one,' he said, dismissing a deep blue silk that she'd bought specially for this trip. 'The simple white one. It's far more you.'

By this time she was beyond argument. In fact, beyond speech.

'I'll call for you in one hour,' he said. Halfway out of the door he looked back, 'By the way, what is your name, please?'

'Sonia,' she said, dazed. 'Sonia Crawford.'

'*Grazie*, Sonia. My name is Francesco Bartini.'

'How kind of you to tell me—finally.'

He grinned. 'Yes, perhaps we should have been formally introduced before you—that is, before I—'

'Get out,' she said, breathing fire. 'Get out while you're still safe.'

'Beautiful *signorina*, I haven't been safe since I opened that door. And nor—I must confess—have you.'

'*Out!*'

'An hour.'

He vanished. At once a light seemed to have gone out of the room. Sonia stared at the door, torn between the impulse to hurl something and an even bigger impulse to yield to the smile that seemed to be taking possession of her whole body.

And the really annoying thing was that she discovered she actually did look best in the simple white dress.

Sonia came out of her reverie to find that she was smiling. However badly their love had ended, it had begun in sunshine and delight. Francesco had been thirty-three then, but so comical and light-hearted that he'd seemed little more than a boy, with a boy's impulsive enthusiasms. Better to remember him like that than as the domestic tyrant he became, or the embittered man of their last meeting.

Nor, however hard she tried, could she silence the voice that whispered the ending hadn't been inevitable, that something better could have grown from that first moment when he'd stared at her nakedness, smiling with admiration.

If she concentrated she could banish the lonely hotel room, and see again his expression, full of shock and the start of longing, feel again the happiness that just the sight of him had once brought her…

She forced herself back to reality. What was the use of thinking like that?

There was a knock on the door, and with a start she realised how much time had passed. This would be Tomaso to fetch her to the hospital. Slowly she went to the door, and opened it.

But it wasn't Tomaso. It was Francesco. And his eyes, as they gazed on her pregnancy, were once again full of shock.

CHAPTER TWO

'*MIO DIO!*' Francesco, murmured, sounding as though he could hardly breathe. '*Oh, mio dio!*'

He came in and shut the door behind him, while his eyes, full of accusation, flew to her face. 'How could you have kept such a thing from me?'

'But—you knew,' she protested. 'Tomaso told you on the phone when he—' The truth hit her like a blow. 'He didn't tell you, did he?'

'Not a word.'

'Oh, how like him! How like this whole family! He spoke Venetian, which he knows I can't follow unless it's very slow. And when he came off the phone he said he'd told you about the baby, and you weren't interested.'

'And you believed *that*?' he demanded.

'Yes, because he said you had someone else, and—oh, this can't be happening!'

'Maybe he thought I had the right to know,' Francesco said in a voice of iron.

She waited for him to say, 'Is it mine?' But he didn't. Like Tomaso, he never doubted the child was his, and she had a brief flicker of the old warmth. These were good people, kind, eager to think the best. Why had she found it so hard to live with them?

'Don't expect me to blame *Poppa*,' Francesco said. 'It's obvious that he had to lie to get you here.'

'And I suppose Giovanna's illness was another invention?'

'No, that's true. My mother's heart is frail. She collapsed a few days ago. She wants me to take you to see her in the hospital.'

She thought of the big bustling woman who had always ruled her family, except for Sonia, who wouldn't let herself be ruled. To Giovanna, every detail of their lives was her domain. The others accepted it as natural and laughed, shrugging it off. But to Sonia, who'd lived alone since she was sixteen, and kept her own counsel even before that, it was intolerable.

Now Giovanna's inexhaustible heart was wearing out. It was like the end of the world.

'You don't mean she's dying?' she asked.

'I don't know. I've never seen her as tired as this before. It's as though all the fight's gone out of her.'

'Your mother—not fighting?'

'Yes,' he said heavily. 'I can't remember a time when she wasn't squaring up to somebody about something. Now she just lies there, and all she wants is to see you.'

'Why? She never liked me.'

'You never liked her.'

'She never wanted me to like her. Oh, look, we can't have this argument again.'

'No, we had it so many times before, didn't we?'

'And it never got us anywhere.'

The fight had carried them through the first few awkward minutes, but now, with round one over, they retired to their corners, and regarded each other warily.

The six months since their last meeting had made him a little heavier and there was a weary look in his eyes that was new, and which hurt her to see. His eyes had always danced—with mischief, with delight. And they had made her too feel like dancing. Now the dancing had stopped and the sun had gone in, and everywhere was cold.

'Where is she?' Sonia asked.

'In the hospital of San Domenico. It's not far.'

In any other city they would have gone by car, but there were no cars in this place where the streets were water, so when they left the hotel they strolled across the piazza before plunging into a maze of tiny alleys.

Sonia pulled her coat about her, shivering. A heavy mist had appeared and in the darkness of the narrow lanes it was hard to see far ahead. All she could make out clearly were the coloured lamps that had been hung up for Christmas, and the lights glowing from the windows of homes. People scurried up and down, carrying parcels, wearing smiles. It was Christmas, and despite the gloomy weather the Venetians were set on celebrating.

A turn brought them out beside a narrow canal, the water's surface pitted by raindrops. Here there were no lights, no people, just a dank chill.

Suddenly she became aware of their direction. 'Not this way,' she said sharply.

'This is the quickest route to the hospital.'

As he spoke they turned another corner and there was the place she hadn't wanted to see, the Ristorante Giminola, looking just the same as when she'd seen it for the first time. Francesco saw her face.

'So you're not as hard-hearted as you would like me to believe,' he said.

If only he knew, she thought, how far from hard-hearted she was. She should never have come back. It hurt too much. She drew a sharp breath. No weakening. She managed to shrug.

'As you say, it's the quickest route to the hospital. Let's go.'

But she walked past the restaurant without looking at it. She didn't want to remember the night when he'd taken her to it for the first time, and they'd fallen in love. That had been two and a half years ago, in another world, where the sun had shone and everything had been possible.

The simple white dress was as perfect on her as he had predicted. She tried on three sets of accessories before settling for a necklace of turquoises mounted in silver.

Then more decisions. Her hair. It was light brown and grew in wavy profusion halfway down her back. Up or down? Of course, he'd already seen it down, that afternoon. Not that he'd been looking at her hair, she recalled with a smile. Up, then.

She studied her face closely, wanting him to see it at its best. She'd been a professional woman ever since she'd first braved the world alone three days after her sixteenth birthday, with no family to help or hinder. She was used to applying make-up to emphasise the assets nature had given her, the lovely skin, regular features and large blue, expressive eyes. But, studying herself in this way, she missed the signs that warned of trouble ahead. Her mouth was curved and lovely, but a touch too resolute, the mouth of a woman who'd had to fight too much, too hard, too young. If she was unlucky it might become stubborn and unyielding, driving away the very thing for which she most yearned.

But right now the warnings were faint. She was in a city she'd dreamed of visiting, full of happy excitement, and her mouth was ready for laughter and—she considered thoughtfully—and whatever else the evening might bring.

At five minutes to the hour there was a knock on her door. Opening it, she found nobody there, just one perfect red rose, lying at her feet. She managed to fix it in her hair, just before the second knock.

This time it was him, and his eyes went straight to the rose.

'Thank you,' he said simply.

She didn't ask where they were going. What did it matter? When they were downstairs he took her hand and led her out into the sunlight, and it was as though she'd never known sunlight in her life before. Across the piazza and into an alley so tiny that the sun was blotted out, around corners, down more alleys, each one looking just like the last.

'How do you ever remember your way?' she asked in wonder.

'I've known the *calles* all my life.'

'*Calles?*' She savoured the word.

'You would call them "alleys", the tiny streets where we can walk and talk to our neighbours.'

Something in his voice made her ask, 'And you love them, don't you?'

'Every brick and stone.'

When they burst out of the last *calle* she had to stand and blink at the flashing of the sunshine on the Grand Canal. Francesco grasped her hand more firmly and drew her to some sheltered tables beside the water. While he ordered coffee she gazed out on the bustle of the canal. Every boat in Venice seemed to be there, and arching over them a wide bridge, with buildings on both sides.

'That's the Rialto Bridge,' Francesco told her. 'Do you remember your Shakespeare? Shylock in *The Merchant of Venice*?'

'He asked, "What news on the Rialto?"' Sonia recalled.

'Because in those days it was a great commercial centre, where all the money deals were done. Now it's mostly trinket shops and a food market.'

'All those boats!' she exclaimed. 'Gondolas, motor boats, all crowded together. You'd think they'd bump into each other. What's that long boat with a white roof?'

'That a *vaporetto*, a kind of bus. It plies the Grand Canal.'

He fell silent while she watched, entranced by the life and the vivid colours. There was so much she wanted to ask about, but not yet. For now it was enough to be here, entranced by the beauty and magic of her surroundings, feeling another, older kind of magic creep over her. She gave him a brief, sidelong glance, but she didn't need to do that to know he was watching her, smiling with delight.

'If you've finished your coffee, we might walk on,' he said at last. As they got to their feet he took her hand again, and led her over the Rialto Bridge.

As he'd said, there was a lively market, just beginning to wind down. He stopped at a stall, took two peaches and handed her one. The plump grocer watched him with a grin, which didn't fade even when Francesco said,

'Your peaches don't get any better. But I'll do you a favour and relieve you of a couple.' He strode on.

'Hey,' Sonia said, hurrying to catch up with him, 'shouldn't you have paid for those?'

'Pay?' he was shocked. 'Pay my own cousin?'

'That man was your cousin?'

'That's Giovanni. Every time his wife gets mad at him he comes to me and I give him a beautiful piece of glass for nothing, to placate her.'

'Does she get mad often?'

He considered. 'He's a good husband—in his way, but he has an eye for the ladies. I'm running out of glass and I haven't paid for my fruit for years.'

She chuckled. This was all mad, but it was like being on another planet, where the rules were different, and she could have a holiday from being her usual tense, cautious self.

Afterwards there were so many things to remember about that first night, but sometimes they all seemed to blur together, and sometimes each detail stood out sharply. All Venice seemed to be the same little street, one turning into another. Yet the Ristorante Giminola where he'd taken her to eat was clear in her mind.

It was a small cosy place where the owner greeted Francesco with a yell and showed them to a table by the window. The menu delighted Sonia. It was printed in three languages and the translations had been done by someone whose English was hit and miss.

'What on earth are "schambed eggs"?' she laughed.

'I think they're "scrambled eggs", but I wouldn't bet on it.'

'And "greem beans"?'

'Done by the same man, I should think. Also "roats potatoes".'

He ordered wine and *prosciutto* ham.

'Tell me about yourself,' he said. 'I want to know everything about you.'

An imp of mischief made her reply, 'I think you've already seen everything about me.'

'Please,' he begged, 'don't remind me of that.'

'Is it such an unpleasant memory?' she teased.

He gave her a speaking look. 'Do you really want me to answer? Well, I shall. But later. When we're alone together.'

She felt as if she was clinging onto a runaway train. Two hours ago she hadn't even met him. Now they were rushing headlong into passion.

But the passion had been there from the moment he saw her nakedness and she saw his shock and admiration. The rest was talk.

'You wanted to know about me,' she said in a voice that wasn't quite steady. 'I'm English. I work for a chain of fancy goods stores—gifts, novelties, fine glass and china. It's just been bought by people who want to expand and they decided to try Venetian glass. They only took over this week, which is why my trip here was arranged at the last minute. It's my first big assignment and I'm going to make a success of it. And it's my first sight of Venice.'

'You put that the wrong way around,' he said gravely. 'It's your first sight of Venice that matters.'

'Well, you're a Venetian—'

'Yes, I'm a Venetian and I know that this is one of the wonders of the world. Now you have seen it, it will be with you all your life.' His merriment had faded, and she realised he was talking about something that mattered to him deeply. She hoped he would go on, but he smiled and said, 'Tell me some more. What about your family?'

'I have none. My parents are both dead. I studied Fine Arts in evening classes, specialising in glass. I want to have a shop with the best glass from all over the world.'

He gave a mock frown. 'But only Venetian glass matters. Why should you bother with any other?'

'Well—other countries do make good glass.'

'Not compared to Venice,' he said firmly.

It was impossible to tell if he was serious, but the gleam was always there in his eyes, and she decided it would be safer to take everything this charmer said with a pinch of salt.

'I think I'll keep my options open,' she said, refusing to be won over so easily.

'Of course you must,' he agreed readily. 'And then you will discover for yourself that Venetian is best.'

'If you say so. Now tell me about you.'

'I am Francesco Bartini. My parents are Tomaso and Giovanna Bartini—'

'And you're their only son,' she said impulsively.

'Of course I'm their only child—except for my brothers Ruggiero, Martino, and Giuseppe.'

'You made that up,' she laughed.

'No, truly. Why did you think I was their only child?'

'You've got so much self-confidence—as though—'

'Spoilt, you mean?' he challenged. 'You could be right. I may not be the only child, but I'm the youngest—and it's almost the same thing.'

'Are you spoilt?' she asked, laughing.

'Rotten. That's why I got out into the world at the first chance and made my own name. I borrowed some money from the bank and bought a disused factory on Murano.'

'Murano?'

'It's one of the islands across the lagoon. They each have their own speciality. With Torcello it's fishing, Burano is lace-making and Murano is glass. The factory had gone out of business but I told the bank manager I could make it work. He didn't believe me—I was only twenty-two—but I talked and talked until he got crazy and said yes to shut me up.'

'I don't believe this,' she laughed. But she did.

Under his gentle questioning she found herself talking about things she'd never discussed before. To say her parents were dead didn't begin to describe the wilderness of pain that had engulfed her when her father walked out on his wife and five-year-old daughter. She'd been alone from that moment, for her mother had collapsed back into herself, and never been the same again. She'd struggled through the next few years, sometimes managing to look after her little daughter, often being looked after by her.

Sonia wasn't even certain that her father was dead. She only knew that she hadn't heard from him for nearly twenty years. Her mother had died when she was twelve leaving a welfare system to take her, more or less kindly, into its care.

'I pity anyone who had me as a foster child,' she told Francesco ruefully. 'I was used to managing my own life and my mother's by that time, and I couldn't stop being bossy. I had three foster homes. They were all glad when I left.'

'I'm sure that's not true.'

It was true, but she didn't try to describe the chaos of her life. The child had developed a fierce independence that she found impossible to give up, and at sixteen she'd been left to confront the world alone, with only her excellent education to help. It had seemed like enough. Beautiful and talented, she'd attracted admiration easily, and if her relationships came and went too quickly, she could dismiss that as the result of her work. She hadn't yet understood that there might be another reason. And on this magic night, when her heart was melting as never before, it was easy to forget that she usually kept it safely guarded.

She talked on and on, rejoicing in the sense of freedom that was new and ecstatic. And suddenly she glanced up to find him watching her, and something caught in her throat. Their eyes held while the world seemed to stop.

After that she'd argued and rationalised, seeking to blind the truth by throwing words in its face. But in her heart she'd known there was no way back.

It was dark when they left the restaurant, and he did what no other man would have done, took her, quite naturally and without self-consciousness, to a tiny little church, tucked away in a back street.

'Come and meet my friend,' he said simply, and Sonia looked around for a priest. Instead he led her to a small niche near the altar where candles burned beneath a figure of a mother and baby.

'When I was a child I started to come here because I liked the Madonna so much,' he confided. 'She's different.'

Sonia saw what he meant. The figure had no trace of the wistful aloofness she'd seen on the faces of other Madonnas. She was plump and cheerful, like a robust little housewife, and she carried a chuckling infant that stretched out his arms to the world.

'I felt she was my special friend and I could talk to her,' Francesco said. 'She listened to my troubles and never disapproved, even when I was bad.'

'Were you very bad?'

'Oh, yes. I kept her working overtime.'

He added a lighted candle to the ones already there, smiled at the little group and gave them a cheeky wink before departing.

'You *winked* at the Madonna?' Sonia said as they left.

'She doesn't mind. She knows it's only me.' He suddenly took her hands. 'I never told anyone about this before. Do you think I'm crazy?'

'No,' she said softly. 'I think it's rather nice.'

Where had they walked after that? She never really knew. Away from the tourist centre, Venice lived in its narrow backstreets. She kept only the memory of their footsteps on the flagstones, the dark narrow *calles*, sparsely lit by lamps so far apart that there was always a pool of darkness halfway between, for lovers.

Somewhere in that darkness he had taken her into his arms and his lips had found hers. It was the culmination of something that had begun that afternoon and she rejoiced at it.

She had never before gone so easily into a man's arms on a first date, but time was rushing swiftly by with the flowing of the water, and magic had to be seized before it vanished. And besides, this was Francesco, who was different to every other man, because his lips were more thrilling and persuasive and made her long for him to hold her tighter.

When he raised his head to study her in the dim light she saw something in his face that made her heart beat faster. He was trembling and she waited for him to draw her closer. But instead he seemed to master himself with an effort.

'We should—go on,' he said.

They wandered on and found themselves by the Grand Canal, with a small flight of steps down to the water. She ventured down, followed by Francesco, determined to kiss her again because his virtuous resolution had already failed. And as they stood, locked in each other's arms, a large boat came up the canal, sending waves streaming to either side, making the water swell about her shoes.

They had cost her a fortune, those shoes, but in that enchanted night, it had all suddenly seemed terribly funny. Oblivious to Francesco's dismayed apologies, she leaned against him, shaking with laughter.

'That was when I fell in love with you,' he'd said on their honeymoon.

'Not until then,' she'd teased. 'What about when you first saw me?'

'No, when I saw you naked and beautiful I was determined to take you to bed. But when you saw the funny side of being soaked my heart became yours, and I decided to marry you.'

'Really? *You* decided?'

'Uh-huh! You never had any choice in the matter. Now, come here.'

Laughing, she'd gone into his arms. It had all been a delightful joke then that Francesco always got what he wanted. What did it matter? She wanted the same things as he, and of course she always would. That went without saying.

CHAPTER THREE

THE next day the Glass Fair began. After breakfast Sonia wandered into the great ballroom of the Cornucopia where last minute preparations were going on, and saw Francesco at once, talking into a mobile. He waved, beckoning her over, and she went, smiling. He wouldn't kiss her in front of this crowd of course, but he would give her a glowing look, meant for only her. Perhaps he would say something special and intimate.

But his first words were, 'If you're going out, can I have your room key so that I can collect what I need?'

'I—yes,' she said, pulling herself together. 'Here it is.'

'Bless you. Did you sleep well?'

'Not very. I was awoken in the night by a box falling on me.'

'That's terrible! Did anything get broken?'

'No, nothing was damaged,' she said with some asperity. 'Including me, thank you for asking!'

He grinned but the phone rang before he could answer. He mouthed, 'Later,' and turned away.

What had she expected? she thought. The lover of the night before was now all businessman. Her time would come—later.

The fair was spread out around five hotels, and Sonia conscientiously visited the other four, talking to salesmen, noting stock, putting in some orders. And all the time she was functioning on automatic. There was a presence in her mind that refused to go away. He just sat there, smiling wickedly at her, reminding her of the night before. Her lips seemed to tingle with the remembered pressure of his, and the anticipation of the evening to come.

By using every ounce of her self-control she managed to put off returning to the Cornucopia until the end of the day, but at last she was free to return. The great ballroom was still busy, for the fair had been a roaring success. Sonia made her way to the Bartini Fine Glass stall, eagerly looking for Francesco.

He wasn't there.

There was a young man in glasses, and two businesslike young women, deep in conversation with customers, but no sign of Francesco.

One of the young women finished with her customer. Sonia showed her business card and said coolly, 'I was hoping to speak to Signor Bartini himself.'

'I'm afraid he's gone for the day. He's taking some clients to dinner.'

It was like a blow in the stomach. He'd just vanished without waiting to see her. Suddenly she felt incredibly foolish. He'd wanted the use of her room and giving her the big romantic act was the simplest way to get it. After all, he was an Italian, wasn't he?

Moonlight, gondolas and magic. But the bottom line was—where else could he have stored all those boxes at a moment's notice?

She hurried up to her room and as she'd expected, every last box had gone. He'd taken what he wanted and left without even a thank you.

She flicked over her notes. She'd done a good day's work and there was no reason for her to stay any longer. The sooner she was out of here the better. She began packing furiously, arranging her clothes with deadly precision. The dress she'd meant to wear for him tonight was folded to within an inch of its life. Having vented her rising temper in this way, she went down to the desk.

'I'd like to check out. Please will you call me a motor boat?'

In a few minutes she was on her way to the station. She would catch the next train and put all this behind her, she decided sensibly.

But at the station she received a check. The last suitable train had left five minutes ago, and the next one wasn't for three hours.

Oh, great! Oh, great!

There was nothing to do but sit on the platform muttering rude words about Francesco, which she did with enthusiasm. She was just starting again from the beginning when a frantic cry of, *'Sonia!'* made her look up to see Francesco tearing along the platform at full speed, arms waving, with the demeanour of a man watching his last hope disappear. She took a moment to enjoy the sight. She felt she'd earned that. Then she rose and faced him wryly.

He pulled up sharply and the words spilled out. 'Where are you going? I've been trying to find you, I've been expecting you all day, and then they told me you'd checked out and I've been going crazy.' It all came out almost in one breath.

'I've spent my day working,' she said indignantly. 'I've been around the whole fair. I called at your stall at the end and was told you'd left for the day. You should be entertaining clients to dinner. What are you doing here?'

'Trying to track down this awkward, prickly woman, who's so dim-witted she can't tell when a man's in love with her. I got through as much work as I could today so that we could spend tomorrow together, *and then you vanished.*'

'*I* vanished? *You* vanished—'

'I left a message at the stall for you to call me—'

'I never got it.'

'And I went up to your room, but it was empty. I

thought I'd lost you, and I ran here…' He took hold of her hands. 'But now I've found you again and I won't let you go.'

He pulled her into his arms and she clung on tightly, overwhelmed with relief and happiness. He kissed her determinedly, just in case there was anything she hadn't understood, and she kissed him back, oblivious to their surroundings and the grins of passers-by.

'You're mad,' she choked. 'Quite mad.'

'I know, darling,' he said into her hair. 'I know.' He picked up her case. 'Let's get back quickly, so that you can change for dinner.'

'But aren't you—?'

'I'm going to take you to meet people, show you off.' He drew her firmly along the platform, never taking his arm from about her waist.

But at her hotel they found a snag. In the short time she'd been gone, her room had already been snapped up.

'That's it,' she said despondently. 'Now I can't stay here.'

'There is somewhere you can go,' he said, almost shyly. 'There's a room in my apartment that nobody's using—'

'I don't think so—'

'You would be as safe as in church. I give you the key to the door and I take many cold showers.'

'Stop talking nonsense,' she said, trying not to laugh.

'You don't want me to take cold showers? That's wonderful! Then we can—'

'No, we *can't*,' she said firmly, yet not without a faint twinge of regret. 'This isn't really a good idea.'

At once he took firm hold of her. 'It's a wonderful idea because I won't let you leave me. Hurry now, we haven't much time.'

'Hey, where are we going?'

'I told you, to my home.' He'd seized up her case and was walking out of the hotel.

He lived in a second floor apartment overlooking a *rio*. It was tiny, kitchen, bathroom, one main room *and only one*—?

'Where's the second bedroom?' she demanded suspiciously.

He looked innocent. 'There isn't one.'

'You said you had a spare room.'

'No,' he said, with the air of a man thinking fast, 'I said I had a room nobody was using just now. And I'm not using it—look, it's quite empty—'

'That's not what—'

'And I'll sleep on the sofa. See, it's easy.'

I was like arguing with a cartload of monkeys. She ought to walk out now. But she didn't want to walk out. Nor did she want to have dinner with his clients. She wanted to stay here and—

'I'll get changed and then we can go out,' she said

firmly. 'Can I have the key to the bedroom door, as you promised me?'

He looked guilty. 'Well, actually—'

'It doesn't lock, does it? Leave at once if you know what's good for you!'

'I take a cold shower,' he said, and vanished quickly.

She was left grinning at the door. She couldn't help it. He was mad. He was tricky. But he was full of life, and at the station he'd said something that had made her heart sing.

'...*so dim-witted she can't tell when a man's in love with her.*'

He was in love with her. But of course it was just another of his tricks and she must be even more on her guard than ever.

When she saw him half an hour later she had to bite back a murmur of admiration. He was in dinner jacket and black bow tie and looked more handsome than any man had the right to.

Tonight she was wearing the dark blue silk dress, the one he'd rejected, but he didn't seem to remember that.

'You are beautiful,' he told her. 'See, I've brought you a gift.'

It was a dainty pendant of silver, so perfect that she gasped. He draped it about her neck and she felt his fingers lightly touch her. But instead of moving away he stayed where he was, his hands on her shoulders, his warm breath whispering against her skin. She too remained quite still, willing him to draw her against him.

'We should leave now,' he said with an effort. 'We mustn't be late.'

'No,' she replied, hardly knowing what she said. Her head was swimming.

They took a motor boat back to the Cornucopia, where Francesco's party was waiting.

'Please forgive me for being late,' he begged, adding, with a grin towards Sonia, 'it's all her fault.'

Everybody laughed and when the introductions had been made they all moved out to the open air restaurant overlooking the Grand Canal, with a view of a floodlit church over the water. Darkness had fallen and the church seemed to be floating, holding Sonia's entranced gaze.

There were eight guests, mostly glass buyers from abroad, plus a couple of Venetians involved in the trade. Sonia sat next to one of these, a man who spoke excellent English, and was soon deep in conversation with him. To her surprised pleasure she found that she could hold her own.

After the meal they left the table and strolled along the balcony. One of the other buyers, an Englishman, came up beside her.

'Heard you talking,' he said smoothly. 'You really know your stuff.'

'Thank you.' She wished he wasn't so close. His aftershave was nearly flattening her.

'I'm the head glass buyer at—' he named London's most luxurious department store. 'Just given Francesco the biggest order he's ever had.'

'I'm sure he deserves it.'

'Well, I believe in encouraging talent. Talking of which, the store is always looking for new blood. I could put a good word in for you.'

'Thank you, but I'm fine where I am.'

He considered a moment before indicating the floodlit church. 'Got nothing like this at home.'

But I'll bet you've got a wife at home, she thought crossly.

'That's true,' she agreed, moving away a little.

He moved closer. 'I get lonely when I'm away. I expect you do, too.'

He raised his hand to trail the fingers along her arm, but his wrist was seized in a hard grip. Francesco's eyes, friendly but implacable, looked directly into his.

'How is that lovely wife of yours, John?'

'She's—er—lovely.' The man flexed his wrist painfully.

'Good. Why don't you call her?'

John attempted a laugh. 'Hey, is that any way to treat your best customer?'

'I sell glass, I don't sell my fiancée.'

John threw up his hands. 'Say no more—mis-understanding—' he sidled away.

Sonia stared at Francesco. 'You said—'

'A figure of speech,' he replied hastily. 'Just to stop him arguing.'

'But he'll cancel his order after the way you treated him. He's your best customer, remember?'

'Yes, he is, and to the devil with him! If he'd touched you any more I'd have thrown him into the canal,' Francesco said deliberately.

'That's very nice of you, but I'm a big girl and I can deal with oafs like him.'

'Don't tell me that,' he complained. 'Tell me how thrilled you were to have me galloping to your rescue on my white charger.'

'No way,' she said stubbornly.

Before he could reply everyone was 'rounded up' by one of the guests who made a speech thanking Francesco for his hospitality, 'and for giving us the chance to meet his lovely bride.'

Sonia opened her mouth, then closed it again.

'I'm sorry,' he said as they were walking home. 'Someone must have overheard me.'

'And taken you seriously.'

'No, it was just an excuse for another drink. Nobody will give it another thought.'

He spoke with a touch of uneasiness that passed her by. She was busy watching the moon appear and disappear between the roofs.

On his doorstep he took her in his arms and kissed her long and lingeringly.

'Wouldn't we be better off doing this inside,' she murmured hazily.

'No, because once inside I cannot touch you again.'

'Why not?'

'Because,' he said in a shaking voice, 'I am a man of honour.'

He wouldn't budge from that. In the privacy of his apartment, with nobody to see what did or didn't happen, he ushered her into her room, bid her a chaste goodnight, and closed the door firmly on her. A few minutes later she heard the sound of the shower going, and smiled even as she thumped the pillow in frustration.

'John' left the next day, having first cancelled his order. Francesco shrugged, handed his exhibition stall over to his assistants, and announced to Sonia that he was taking her on a visit to his factory.

'Your employers will be most impressed that you've investigated real Venetian glass-making,' he promised her. 'What's the matter?'

'Nothing,' she said, looking about her. 'Except that I thought there was a woman over there, watching us.'

Francesco glanced up just in time to see the woman retreat into the shadows.

'Never mind,' he said, hurrying her along.

'There's someone else watching us on the other side.'

'I know. I saw.'

'But who are they?'

'The first one was my Aunt Celia, and the second was my niece Bettina. You've already met Giuseppe. Forget them. There'll be plenty more.'

'They're spying on us?'

'In Venice it's not called spying. It's called taking a family interest. The man leaning out of the window over there is my eldest brother Ruggiero.'

'You mean—last night—?'

'It's all over Venice by now,' he admitted. 'Baby brother has gotten himself engaged at last.'

'But we're not really—I mean it was only—'

'There's a boat,' he said hastily. 'Run.'

Seizing her hand he hurried to the jetty where a water taxi had just pulled in. The driver hailed him by name, and said, 'Murano, eh?' without waiting to be told. It was obvious Francesco was well known all over Venice.

The island of Murano lay across the lagoon. As the wind streamed through her hair Sonia had the feeling of travelling directly into the sunlight. It was all about her, glittering on the water, dancing in the distance, inviting her on to somewhere beautiful and exciting that she'd never dreamed of before. She laughed aloud, looking in Francesco's eyes, and reached out her hand to him.

The factory was like a furnace, a place where the traditional methods of glass-making were treasured.

She watched, entranced, as a man created a vase by blowing, turning the pipe around and around. She didn't even notice another man, rapidly sketching her as she watched, but later there was a plaque with her own head etched on it. The perfect end to a perfect visit. Had she felt, even then, that it was too perfect, too romantic, too *much*? Or had she walked on, blinded by enchantment?

There had been so little enchantment in her life. Did she really blame herself for yielding in a weak moment, or regret those few days of blazing, heart stopping happiness?

They returned to the main part of Venice for lunch, wandering through the streets until they found a place to eat. And everywhere Sonia realised that she was being inspected. Once a beautiful dark-skinned young woman waved and vanished quickly.

'My sister-in-law, Wenda,' Francesco explained. 'She's Jamaican.'

'And I suppose you're also related to the oriental girl studying us from behind that stall,' Sonia retorted.

She'd spoken ironically but Francesco replied, 'That's Lin Soo. She's from Korea and she's married to my Uncle Benito.'

She burst out laughing. 'Have any of your family married Venetians?'

'One or two. But we tend to go travelling and bring brides home. When we all sit down together it's like the United Nations.'

They ate in a tiny *trattoria*, whose owner—as Sonia was growing used to—hailed him by name.

'It's as though you knew everyone in Venice,' she said in wonder.

'But I do,' he said in surprise. 'I've lived here all my life.'

'I've lived all my life in London, but I don't know everyone there.'

'That's because London's a huge city. Venice is called a city, because it's one of the great treasures of the world, but it's actually a small village. If you know the way you can walk from one end to the other in half an hour, and meet your friends around every corner.'

As they were drinking coffee his mobile rang. The subsequent conversation consisted mostly of Francesco saying, *'Si, Poppa—si, Poppa!'* When he had finished he said, 'I'm under orders to take you home to supper tonight.'

'Your father's orders?'

'Goodness no! My mother's. He was just acting as her messenger.'

She was amused. 'Suppose I have other ideas?'

'*I* had other ideas, but when Mamma speaks, we all jump.' He saw her regarding him with her head on one side, and he looked uneasy. 'It's better we do as my mother says.'

'All right, as long as you take me there in a gondola.'

'But a gondola isn't a method of transport,' he explained. 'They do round trips for the tourists.'

'You mean you don't have a gondolier friend who'll make an exception for you?' she teased.

And, of course, he did. Marco had been to school with Francesco, and gladly made a special trip for him.

'How can he row this thing with just one oar?' Sonia wanted to know. 'We ought to be going around in circles.'

'One side of the boat is longer than the other,' Francesco told her, straight-faced.

'Oh, really—'

'Honestly. It bulges more one side than the other, and that evens it out. It's like everything else in Venice, like the Venetians themselves. Cock-eyed!'

She began to laugh. He laughed with her, and somehow her head was on his shoulder as they floated onwards to the Rio di St. Barnaba, where his parents lived.

Marco helped them disembark, looking Sonia over with admiration, then watched them stroll out of sight before whipping out his mobile to spread the news that another good man had bitten the dust.

Now the gondolas were still. On the Grand Canal the *vaporetti* chugged noisily up and down. Christmas was nearly here, and last minute preparations were in full swing, yet the streets were strangely peaceful. No vehicles, only people, smiling, stopping to talk to each other, breaking off the shopping for a quick visit to a bar.

There was a bar on the corner, casting its glow over the dim light of the street, luring them with sounds of good cheer.

'I usually stop here for a coffee first,' Francesco said.

'Fine,' she said, glad to defer the coming meeting.

A light snow was beginning to fall as they slipped inside and she settled at a table while he brought them coffee. Italian bars were unlike American bars or British pubs. As well as wine and beer, they sold coffee, ice cream and cakes, and were places where the whole family enjoyed themselves together.

Today this one was busy with people crowded around little tables, toasting each other with cries of *'Buon natale'* and *'Bon nadal.'*

'How happy they look,' she murmured wistfully.

A burst of laughter from a table in the corner made her look more closely, frowning, for she was sure she recognised her sister-in-law, the Korean Lin Soo.

Soo, as the family called her, had with her two children of about ten, their faces a beautiful mixture of Italian and oriental, their eyes dark and excited. They beamed when they saw her and hurried to throw their arms about her. 'Aunt Sonia!'

Then Soo came to embrace her, and behind her Teresa, Giuseppe's wife.

'We've just come from visiting Mamma,' they told her. 'We always stop here afterwards.'

The needless explanation told its own story. Sonia gave Francesco a wry look, which he met with bland innocence.

'What a coincidence,' she murmured. But she was really glad to see these two, whom she'd always liked. They settled down to talk about Mamma and the giddy spell—not a heart attack, they were quick to insist—that had taken her to hospital.

'We thought she'd be out after a few days' rest,' Soo mourned, 'but she just lies there, as though she's too tired to go on.'

With almost deafening tact they failed to mention her pregnancy, and Sonia guessed that Tomaso had warned them. Once more the mobile connections had been humming, spinning a web of anticipation about her, so that wherever she went there was a Bartini waiting. Once she had found it suffocating, but now she was grateful not to have to make explanations. There was, after all, something restful about people who knew and accepted you without question, and worried about you when you weren't there.

After a few minutes her sisters-in-law departed, despite Francesco's urging them to stay.

'Don't stop them,' Sonia said when they'd gone,

adding, amused, 'They have to call *Poppa* and tell him that we're nearly here.'

'I already did that while you were talking,' he confessed.

After a moment she laughed. 'It's like being under surveillance by the CIA,' she said.

'But not spied on,' he said quickly. 'Watched over. They're all thrilled that you're here. Of course good news gets passed on.'

She preferred not to answer this directly. 'I remember the night you took me to meet them all. They were strange to me, but every one of them knew what I looked like. Everywhere we went in Venice there was a Bartini watching us and reporting back. I've never known a grapevine like it.'

'My father was especially anxious to meet you. Both Ruggiero and Giuseppe had told him how beautiful you were.'

'He was always nice to me,' she remembered with a smile.

When she remembered that meeting, Tomaso was the one she saw first, a little, bald-headed man, beaming all over his round face, advancing with arms out-stretched, greeting her as a daughter, although she hadn't yet agreed to marry Francesco. She wasn't even thinking of it, she told herself.

And behind him, Giovanna, large, magisterial, her face set in an expression of welcome that didn't quite disguise its natural aloofness.

They were all there, and with the Bartinis *all* was a big word. As well as his brothers and their wives there were Tomaso's siblings, and Giovanna's. At various points in the evening miscellaneous nephews and nieces found excuses to drop in, greet Sonia, look her over, and smile a welcome. Once she reckoned there were as many as thirty people in the tiny place.

Tomaso spoke some English but Giovanna had none. Wenda acted as interpreter while Giovanna fired questions at her as though from a machine gun. Under such circumstances it just wasn't possible to explain that she and Francesco weren't really engaged. She did her best, stressing that they'd only met two days ago, but that only provoked Tomaso to recall that he'd fallen in love with Giovanna at first sight, too.

They ate in the pocket-sized garden, hung with coloured lamps. The meal was magnificent, course after course of perfectly prepared Venetian dishes, until she felt overwhelmed.

Perhaps that was the idea, she thought. Giovanna was watching her, but so were all the others. It seemed that everyone had contributed to the meal, and they all scurried back and forth to and from the kitchen. But their smiles were so genuine and their pleasure in her company so frank that she soon relaxed and forgot that she was 'on show'. When she left they each kissed her and murmured something about seeing her again soon, and she murmured something vague in return.

They were all crowded at the doors and windows to wave her farewell. At the corner of the street she turned and waved back, feeling as if all the world was there, smiling at her. At an upper window Giovanna stood alone.

CHAPTER FOUR

BY NOW Sonia was becoming used to the Venetian grapevine, so it didn't seem strange that when they turned the corner there was Marco and his gondola, waiting for them.

'Is he going to take us back to your apartment?' she asked with a smile.

'And a few other places first.'

It was late at night and most of Venice had gone to bed, so they had the little canals almost to themselves. Only one or two other gondolas were out, and for the first time Sonia heard the yodelling cries that gondoliers uttered when approaching a blind corner, to warn other traffic. In the warm night air those cries echoed back and forth across the water until they whispered away into the silence. She listened, entranced by the sound, by Venice, by her love.

'I have to go home tomorrow,' she said from within the crook of Francesco's arm.

'Why?'

'I've stretched this visit as long as I can. It began as a working trip and it turned into a holiday.'

He didn't reply, seeming sunk in thought. He knew now that this was the end of their time together. Tonight they would set the seal on a beautiful holiday romance that she would remember all her life.

Because that was all it was, all it could ever be: a holiday romance. To think anything else was madness.

By now she thought she knew Francesco, a light-hearted charmer, full of tricks, able to turn any situation to his own account. But he was also, as he'd told her, a man of honour, and unexpectedly stubborn about it. When they reached home, tonight was the same as last night, the chaste kiss, the bedroom door safely closed on her.

It was up to her, then.

She waited until the night was quiet before slipping out of the bedroom and into the main room where he lay sleeping on the sofa, a blanket thrown over him. She could just see his face. In sleep it had an innocence at variance with his wicked charm. Dropping to one knee beside him she laid her mouth over his.

After a moment he opened his eyes and she felt his arms go about her. This was different from kisses they'd shared in shadowed alleyways. It was full of

purpose as though he'd come to an inevitable con-
clusion. She stood up, taking his hand in hers, and
led him into the bedroom.

Now he knew that she wanted him he threw off
restraint as easily as he threw off the few clothes he
was wearing, and eased her nightdress down from
her shoulders so that it slipped to the floor, leaving
her naked and lovely.

His first kisses on her neck and breasts were
gentle, almost by way of introducing himself, then
more urgent as he felt her flower under his touch.
With a sense of blissful release she let go of caution.
There would be another time to be cautious, but
now was a time to love, even if only fleetingly.

Love should always be like this. Here was a poi-
gnancy of emotion and sensation that might never
come to her again, so she would treasure it in her
heart. She would remember too the way he touched
her body as though she were the first and only woman
in the world, and whispered strange, passionate
words that she understood only through their inten-
sity.

In the hot summer night they made love with the
windows flung open so that the sound of softly
flowing water streamed into her consciousness and
seemed to carry her away. The moonlight limned his
body, covering hers, but she was less aware of the
sight of him than of the feel of pleasure and joy deep
within. His caresses were skilled, but they touched

her heart less than the near reverence with which he treated her, as though he was afraid she might vanish from his arms at any moment.

Afterwards, as they lay close, he murmured gently to her in words she didn't understand.

'What was that?'

'Te voja ben. Te voja ben.'

'What does it mean?' she whispered against his skin.

'It's how a Venetian says "I love you."'

Silence. He was waiting for her to say it too, but was she out of her mind? She barely knew him. She should flee this minute, back to her old, safe life.

'Te voja ben,' she whispered.

She hadn't meant to say it, and as soon as the words were out she knew she should take them back. But she couldn't. She had known perfection, and she wouldn't insult it with regrets.

'Te voja ben.' She framed the words again as she fell asleep.

She awoke to the sound of Francesco busy in the kitchen. She lay listening to him for a moment, smiling at her memories. But hard on their heels came the remembrance that this was the end.

'I'll get packing right away,' she said over breakfast.

'Of course,' he said readily.

Too readily, she thought, with a sinking heart. Surely after last night he had something else to say?

'It'll be enough if you catch the afternoon train,' he observed. 'This morning we can go for a walk.'

He took her along the waterfront with palaces on one side and the shining lagoon on the other until they reached the park known as the Garibaldi Gardens. Down the centre was a wide avenue of trees, lined with stone benches forty feet apart. He led her to one of these and they sat quietly together, while time passed, and still he said nothing.

At last he spoke. 'I'm sorry if Mamma overwhelmed you last night.'

'It was you, telling her that we were going to get married.'

'I didn't exactly tell her,' he protested. 'Just—'

'You just told everyone.'

'That's true. And Mamma picked up the idea because it's so much what she wants. Now she's set her heart on it.'

'Well, I'm sure you can explain after I've gone.'

He looked alarmed. 'But, darling, I always do what Mamma wants.'

It took a moment for this to sink in. 'What—are you saying?'

He looked pathetic. 'If I don't marry you, she'll beat me up. You wouldn't want that, would you?'

'Oh—*you*!' Laughing, she aimed a swing at him, but he imprisoned her arms.

'Oh, no,' he said firmly. 'If *you* want to beat me up, you have to marry me first. It's a family privilege.'

She was on the point of throwing herself into his arms when she was suddenly swamped by an attack of common sense. Normally common sense was her element, but it had been so much in abeyance recently that it returned now with the force of a gale.

'We can't do this,' she said hurriedly. 'We're crazy to be even thinking about marriage. We know nothing about each other.'

'We know that we love each other.'

'You don't know me. I'm not the person you've seen the last few days—laughing, relaxed, just letting things happen. I *never* just let things happen to me. I always plan, so that I've got some control. I feel safer that way. But here, with you, I'm different.'

'But that's good—'

'I'm different because I'm on holiday,' she cried. 'But when I'm me again I'm—someone else. Someone you might not even like.'

Why, oh, why hadn't he listened to her? she thought long afterwards. For she'd been right in every word, as though she'd had a ray of clairvoyance.

But instead of being sensible he'd looked at her and said gently, 'Are you saying you don't love me?'

'No—no, I *do* love you—'

'Then the rest can be sorted out.'

She hadn't the heart to protest further. She wanted him too much, and in this lovely place it was easy to believe that all problems had an answer.

'*Te voja ben,*' he repeated. 'I love you.'

She wrinkled her brow. 'Which word means "love"?'

'None of them. Literally it is, "I wish you well."' He seized tight hold of her. 'I wish you well, Sonia.' Then, head thrown back, a triumphant shout up to heaven. '*I wish you well.*'

She began to laugh, not with amusement but with joy. He joined in and everything was laughter and happiness.

'Say yes,' he cried. 'Say it quickly before you have time to think. Say it, say it.'

'Yes,' she laughed. 'Yes, *yes, YES!*'

'Come!' he seized her hand and began to run.

'Where are we going?' she gasped, struggling to keep up.

'To tell my family. They'll be so pleased.'

'But—'

'Hurry, it'll take hours to visit them all.'

And it did, she thought later. *Even at that moment, he thought of the family first.*

But still, it was the happiest day I ever had.

Now here they were, little more than two years later, further apart than they had ever been as they walked side by side to the hospital to see his mother. The cold seemed to be in her heart, yet at the same time, it seeped into her from the outside: not crisp, bracing cold such as she'd known in England, but damp, depressing cold.

'This must be the most miserable city in the world in winter,' she said, shivering.

'No place is at its best in winter.'

'But the others don't have this much water. It's everywhere, all around you, and it makes everything so dank. I always disliked Venice in winter.'

'Yes, you were never a true Venetian,' he agreed. 'We love our home best now, because when the tourists have gone we have time for each other. But you never had time for any of us.'

'I was never given the choice. It was as though the whole family lived together. All fifty, or was it sixty? Your mother even chose where you and I should live.'

'My bachelor flat was too small for us. And you liked the new place until you realised *she'd* found it.'

'And it was only two streets away from her.'

'Venice is a tiny place. You're never more than a few streets away from anyone.' He added heavily, 'Well, you're far enough away now, aren't you?'

A few minutes more brought them to the hospital of San Domenico. It was a small place but finely equipped, and the white corridors looked pleasant and cheerful, especially now, hung with brilliant

Christmas decorations. The way up to Giovanna's room lay past Maternity, and as they neared the door a plump little nun came briskly out, clutching a wad of files. Her face lit up as she saw Sonia's bulge.

'There, I knew I'd win!' she said, beaming. 'I'm Mother Lucia. I run the Maternity Ward. You're just in the nick of time.'

'For what?' Sonia asked, bewildered.

'Why, to have our Christmas baby of course. I bet Dr Antonio that we'd have one.'

'You took a *bet*?' she echoed, unable to keep her eyes from the little nun's habit.

Mother Lucia chuckled, understanding everything Sonia couldn't say. 'I bet him three chocolate bars, that we'd have a Christmas baby,' she said, 'but he insisted there was nobody due. He must have forgotten about you.'

'No, I'm not a patient here,' Sonia said hurriedly. 'I'm visiting from England.'

'Oh!' The little nun's face fell with almost comical disappointment.

'Besides, I'm only eight months gone.'

'Rather more, I should have thought,' Mother Lucia said, regarding her judiciously. 'I think I might win yet. I'll light a candle to our Madonna downstairs. She often solves problems.'

Sonia had grown used to the Italian way of regarding the Madonna less as a religious icon than as a friendly aunt, but even so she was left gaping by this practical speech. Mother Lucia gave a last speculative look at her pregnancy before bustling away.

Giovanna was in a room on the second floor, lying still, her hand in Tomaso's. He was sitting beside her, his eyes fixed on her face. Now and then he patted her hand gently and looked into her face for some sign of a reaction. But she seemed unaware of him, her eyes fixed on some distant world inside herself. Sonia thought she had never seen an expression more piteous than Tomaso's as he tried to recall her to him, perhaps before she slipped away forever.

He looked up and smiled briefly, coming towards them.

'I ought to be angry with you,' she told Tomaso. 'You told me you'd explained to Francesco about—' she indicated her bump.

Tomaso gave a shrug, very Venetian. 'Sometimes it's good to tell the truth,' he said wisely. 'Sometimes—better don't bother. She'll be so glad you came,' he hurried on before Sonia could speak. 'The others have all been in, but it's you she asks for.'

Sonia went to the bed, and was shocked to see how frail Giovanna looked. She had always been a big woman, tall and broad shouldered, with the air of someone who could cope with the whole world. Now she seemed to have shrunk. She opened her eyes and looked at Sonia.

'You came,' she murmured, sounding surprised.

'Of course,' Sonia replied, not really knowing what to say.

'I thought you—refuse,' Giovanna said, speaking in her fractured English.

'No, I came as soon as I knew you wanted me,' Sonia said. It wasn't strictly true, but Tomaso was right. Sometimes it was better not to bother with the truth.

'Bad you go away,' Giovanna murmured. 'Better for me to go—I did harm, but—not mean to.'

'It wasn't you,' Sonia said. 'It was me. Our marriage was wrong from the start. Francesco can find someone who suits him better.'

'Better than wife he loves?' Giovanna asked. 'Better than his child's mother?' She hadn't previously reacted to the pregnancy, but she'd noticed it, Sonia now realised.

'You don't know—' Giovanna murmured.

'What don't I know?'

'A baby—changes everything. Nothing is the same—love is not the same. But *you* do not love *him*, eh?'

'No—maybe—I don't know.'

'My fault,' Giovanna said with a sigh of exhaustion. 'I tried to—but no good. Too late.'

'I don't understand you.'

'How can you? Long, long time ago.' She sighed. 'No matter now.'

'But it does matter,' Sonia said, alerted by something in the old woman's manner. Giovanna was trying to tell her something and she didn't understand. They had never understood each other. 'Try to tell me.'

Suddenly Giovanna's hand tightened on Sonia's, and a terrible urgency came over her. 'Not—like—me,' she said vehemently.

'I do like you,' Sonia lied. 'Or I could have done, if—'

'No!' Giovanna's face was contorted with effort. 'Not that—'

But it was too much for her. She released her grip and fell back against her pillows, her eyes closed.

'I'm sorry,' Sonia said to Tomaso and Francesco. 'I'm afraid I've tired her.'

'You did your best,' Tomaso said. 'You came here.'

Full of pity for the old woman, Sonia leaned over to kiss her, and was close enough to hear the soft murmur, *'No esser come mi.'*

She stared, but Giovanna lay still, and she couldn't be certain that she'd heard anything. She turned away, feeling despondently that her visit here had been a total failure.

As they walked away from the hospital, Francesco put his arm around her shoulder and said gently, 'Thank you, that was kind.'

'Will she die, do you think?'

'I don't know. I hope not. But if so, she will go more peacefully for having spoken to you.'

Sonia was silent, thinking things weren't that simple. Her failure to connect with Giovanna had given her a sense of floundering that was only too familiar. The old woman's last message had been spoken in Venetian, and she simply hadn't understood it.

'Perhaps you'll come and see her again before you go?' he said.

'I don't think so. I'm starting back tomorrow morning.'

'So soon? I thought—that is, I hoped—'

'I can't stay. I've done what I came to do, and I need to get back home.'

'But, in your state, should you take that long journey again?'

'I'll have a good night's sleep.'

He shrugged. 'Well then, you'd better clear out the last of your things.'

'What?'

'You left some stuff at the flat. I don't like to throw it out unless you tell me, but I need the space.'

For his new girlfriend, she thought. Well, that was all right.

'I didn't know I'd left anything behind. You never said.'

He shrugged. 'I suppose I got a bit sentimental about them. But it's water under the bridge, isn't it? You'd better come and see to it now.'

'Right,' she said cheerfully. 'Let's get it done.'

As he said, the time for sentiment was past. She would clear the last of her things out of the apartment, and they could both start the process of forgetting.

Her feet remembered the path to the little *rio*, then down this tiny street and into a turning that only those in the know realised was there. And there was the little canal and the short walk along its bank to the oak door.

Nothing had changed since she first entered this building, her arms full of things for the kitchen, her head full of plans for redecorating, only to find that the family had already worked out a colour scheme. It was a good scheme, she had to admit, and she would have liked it a lot if she and Francesco had worked it out together. But it had been Giovanna's idea, with Tomaso's help. Benito had obtained cheap materials from the shop where he worked, and Wenda was able to get a bargain on the perfect curtain fabric. There had been nothing for Sonia to do except host the party where they all looked around and congratulated themselves and each other. And even then Giovanna had baked the cakes.

The memories, with their burden of resentment, came back to her as she climbed the stairs to the upper floor where they had lived. Everything was the same, including the kitchen; modern cooking equipment, surrounded by beautiful blue and white tiles and hung with copper pans.

She looked around the flat, seeking signs of his new lover. But all she found was her own wedding picture, just where it had always stood on the sideboard, the bride and groom dazzlingly young and happy.

'Doesn't she mind you keeping that there?'

'Doesn't who mind?'

'Your new friend. *Poppa* said you were courting someone else.'

Some changed quality in the silence made her turn to find him regarding her more coldly than she'd ever seen.

'Don't be so stupid,' he said angrily.

She drew a sharp breath understanding what she should have realised before. Of course, it had been another of Tomaso's inventions to get her here.

'I should have thought—*Poppa*—'

'I suppose he knew you wouldn't come unless you felt safe from me,' Francesco said bitterly, and turned away to the kitchen. Sonia stayed where she was, trying to come to terms with the senseless happiness that had swamped her. He didn't love anyone else. Then she put a brake on her thoughts. What difference could it make to her now?

After a moment she followed him into the kitchen.

'I'm sorry,' he said at once. 'I shouldn't have gotten mad at you. Are you all right?' His eyes were on her pregnancy.

'Yes, I'm fine. I'm not going to collapse just because you were a bit cross. I've sailed through this pregnancy with less trouble than most women have.'

'Well, that's nice.' His smile was strained, reminding her that she was telling him something he should have been there to see for himself.

What could she say to him, she wondered, when every remark concealed a minefield?

'When did you know about the baby?' he asked her.

'Soon after you left England that last time. When I left here, I had no idea at all.'

'I wonder what you would have done if you had,' he murmured.

'I don't know. I never let myself think of "if only". What's the point?'

'There might be a point,' he mused. 'We might learn where we went wrong.'

'But we know that. We've always known. It was me. It's a wonderful life here, everyone so warm and involved with each other. I just can't be that way. I don't know how to be so close. I tried to warn you once—or warn myself.' She gave a short laugh. 'I didn't listen to myself, did I?'

'Perhaps you didn't want to.'

'That's right, I didn't. I wanted to believe your pretty fantasy of everything being all right if we loved each other enough. You once called me a cold woman who prefers to live isolated—'

'I never said that,' he protested quickly.

'You did. In one of our last quarrels—how many did we have in those final days?'

'It doesn't matter. I don't recall them. I only think of you as I fell in love with you, sweet and generous, and laughing.'

'That wasn't me, only my holiday self. She doesn't exist any more. I never laugh now.'

'You need me to make you laugh,' he said gently.

She smiled. 'Yes, you could always do that.'

He returned to the stove where something was simmering. 'What are you making?' she asked.

'How about "schambed eggs"?' he asked, with an attempt at lightness.

'And "greem beans"' she capped it, also trying to sound cheerful.

But it was no use. The pretence of cheerfulness couldn't last. After a moment he went into another room and emerged with a cardboard box.

'Better have a look through these,' he said shortly.

There was nothing valuable in the box, just silly little things. But somehow the story of their love was in those silly little things. Here was the cheap wooden brooch he'd bought her from a market stall on the day she returned to Venice for their marriage. It was worth about fourpence, but he'd presented it to her with great solemnity, announcing that this was her wedding present so she mustn't expect another. And they'd giggled like mad things, and been happy.

His real wedding gift had been a pearl necklace that she'd worn with her bridal gown, but the wooden brooch had been pinned beneath her dress, where only the two of them knew of it.

She had gone to her wedding in a gondola decked with flowers, like a traditional Venetian bride. Since she had no family Tomaso had given her away, beaming with pride as he handed her into the rocking boat and helped adjust her white satin dress and long veil. The gondolier had warbled a song of love as he ferried them along the Grand Canal to the Church of San Simeone. At the last moment they had glided under the Academia Bridge and a cascade of flowers had fallen from a crowd of children leaning eagerly over the railing above.

On the steps of the church Tomaso had helped her out, and the gondolier had kissed her cheek for luck. It had all been too lovely to be true.

Too lovely to be true.

Nobody should marry like that, she'd thought often since. *Sensible brides should pick a dreary civic office on a cold winter day, not let themselves be enchanted by flowers and music and beauty.*

And by a young man standing tall and upright, the laughter driven from his eyes by love. But Sonia quickly shut that thought off. How long could love last when it was built on illusion?

CHAPTER FIVE

THERE were more 'treasures' in the box, a stack of goodwill cards welcoming the newest Bartini; for that was how the family had seen it. She was becoming a Bartini, and abandoning anything else she might have been. They had never understood that she hadn't seen it that way.

Other women, with her lonely background, would have loved the welcome and melted happily into the family that was so eager to have her.

But I had to be awkward, she thought, despairingly. I felt suffocated.

'Why do we always have to have Sunday dinner with the family?' she'd demanded once, not too long after their marriage.

'But weekends are when we can all get together,' he'd said, baffled. 'They love having you.'

More cards congratulating her on being pregnant, and yet more, little funny teasers to cheer her up when it proved a false alarm.

'Why did you have to tell everyone?' she'd stormed. 'I was only a week late. There was no need for anyone to know.'

'I wanted them to share our happiness. Now they want to comfort you.'

She couldn't tell him that she didn't need comforting. The thought of a baby so soon had made her feel suffocated and she'd been secretly relieved at the chance to wait a little longer. But she couldn't say that to Francesco, the warm-hearted family man. And there were so many things she couldn't say to him, she came to realise.

She returned to the box and found a small booklet about Bartini Fine Glass, produced for tourists in several languages. The English version was like the menus, full of howlers. They had laughed over it together, and she'd enjoyed doing her first job for him, correcting the English so that it was perfect.

It was all going to be so easy. They had everything planned. She was a glass expert, he was a glass manufacturer. They would work wonderfully well together. But the blunt fact, as she realised in the first week, was that Francesco didn't need a glass expert. He already knew what he was doing, and that was producing fine Venetian glass in a centuries-old tradition. Sonia's ability to place his product in the context of the rest of the art world didn't help turn out more vases.

She was at her best when helping him to entertain customers. Then her knowledge was an asset. But even a successful manufacturer didn't entertain customers every night, and in between times there was little for her to do. She couldn't help with his paperwork because it was in Italian, which she didn't understand. Her one great talent which was useful in the factory, was as a packer. She packed very neatly. But she was the boss's wife, and it raised eyebrows.

'It'll be better, darling, when you've learned the language,' he said soothingly.

'What language?' she demanded crossly. She was smarting from the unaccustomed sense of inadequacy. All her life she'd been able to do whatever she set her mind to, and this new experience was hard to cope with.

'What use is Italian?' she demanded now. 'You all speak Venetian dialect.'

'Then learn Venetian,' he said, sounding exasperated with her for the first time.

But Venetian drove her crazy. In her ignorance she had assumed that a dialect was little more than a different accent on the odd word, but this 'dialect' was a whole new language, filled with the letter 'j', a letter Italian had never heard of.

It ended with her leaving the firm to acquire the language skills she needed. Italian, Venetian, German, and French, of which she already had a smattering.

For the first time since she was sixteen she had no job to go to. For Italian and Venetian she went out to lessons, but for French and German she studied at home.

'Trapped,' she said to herself once. 'Trapped at home like a housewife.'

She reassured herself that soon it would be over, when she acquired the necessary skills. But she had no aptitude for languages and the work came hard to her. Often she felt she was floundering in a quagmire, with no hope of escape. The walls of her home began to seem like a prison.

Worse was everyone's assumption that since she stayed at home she had infinite leisure. Everyone dropped in just when they felt like it, and expressed surprise that she didn't drop in on them. Wenda, Ruggiero's wife, confided to Sonia that she loved Venice because it was just like the village in Jamaica where she'd been born.

Seeing Sonia's look of surprise, she explained, 'It's small, you walk everywhere, and people are friendly.'

Giovanna came constantly, apparently to talk but actually, Sonia suspected, to cast her eagle eyes over the domestic arrangements and find fault with them. Not that she ever openly criticised, but it seemed to Sonia that her offers of help were an unspoken criticism.

She even learned to speak a sort of English,

something she had never done for her other daughters-in-law. In Sonia's heightened state of sensitivity it seemed like the final insult.

'She's just trying to be kind,' Francesco argued. 'It can't be easy to learn a new language at her age, but she wants to communicate with you.'

'Does she? Or does she want to underline how useless I am? She can learn a new language at her age, but I can't learn one at mine. That's the message.'

'I'm sure it isn't. We all know English is easier to learn than anything else because of its simple grammar.'

'Then why didn't she learn it for Wenda instead of waiting for Wenda to learn Italian and Venetian? Because Wenda can manage languages and I can't.'

If Giovanna arrived when Sonia was studying she would ostentatiously look around for any housework that hadn't been done, and proceed to do it. Soon she knew enough English to tell Sonia to get back to her studying and leave everything to her. Which left Sonia feeling as though she'd been blamed for some unspecified crime.

'She even rearranges the china,' she complained to Francesco in frustration. 'She washes up, then puts things where *she* wants them.'

'She thinks of *you* as the one who rearranges the china,' Francesco said. 'She just puts it back the way I always had it.'

'And how did you decide how you wanted it?'

He gave a rueful grin. 'Mamma did it.'

'Exactly. Nobody's allowed to disagree with Mamma.'

A strange look came over his face. 'Don't let's quarrel about my mother,' he begged.

Only later did she realise that his words had contained a warning.

The one thing that she had never been able to discuss with him, and which baffled her to this day, was the truly subtle way Giovanna had undermined her by refusing to call her by her proper name.

She could trace it back to the day just before the wedding when Giovanna had chanced to see her passport, bearing the full name, Sonia Maria Crawford.

'Maria,' she said in a wondering tone. Then, as if she'd discovered something vital, 'Maria!'

'No, Sonia.' Sonia pointed to her first name. 'Sonia,' she repeated firmly.

But thereafter, whenever they were alone, Giovanna had addressed her as Maria. It was a small point, but it became more important as her feeling of being a fish out of water had increased. This society was so intent on swallowing her alive that she wasn't even to be allowed her own name.

Francesco was baffled by her objection.

'I've never heard her call you Maria,' he said truthfully.

'That's because she only does it when there's nobody else there. Why?'

His attempt to broach the subject with his mother had been a disaster. Giovanna had reddened, rapped out something in Venetian, and stormed out, slamming the door.

'She says she doesn't know what you're talking about,' Francesco explained. 'Are you sure you're not imagining this?'

'No, I'm not imagining this,' she said, glaring. 'But if you're just going to take her side there's no more to be said.'

'Why do I have to take sides?' he demanded angrily. 'Why are you always at odds with my family?'

'Because they won't let you go,' she cried. 'And you don't really want them to.'

'Nonsense. You just don't understand. It's called family closeness.'

'It's called being the youngest son and making the most of it!'

'I can't help being the youngest son.'

'You told me once you asserted your independence by getting out of the house and starting the business. But inside you you're still there.'

'I love my family. I can't help it. And I don't want to have to make choices.'

When had she decided to leave? The question was unanswerable because she never really had decided.

'I need a bit of time to myself,' she said to him one day. 'Just let me go to England for a little while and—we'll see.'

He'd made no objection. But when, after a month, he'd followed her and demanded point blank that she return, the result had been a fierce quarrel. Even that might have ended differently if he hadn't made the mistake of saying,

'I thought by now you'd have seen sense.'

She gasped. 'You haven't understood a word I've said, have you? To you it's just been one big sulk until I "see sense".'

'Well, hasn't it?'

It had gone of from there, spiralling from anger to more anger, until he'd stormed off. The next day she'd discovered that this time she really was pregnant. But from Francesco there was only silence.

As she grew bigger she'd known that soon she must come to a resolution, but she'd always put off the day. Now the resolution had been forced on her, and she tried to tell herself that she was glad.

'Ready?' Francesco asked, wielding plates.

His cooking was delicious, and perfectly judged.

'Something light because you don't want any dead weights on your stomach just now,' he said.

'How many expectant mothers have you cooked for?'

'Loads. All my sisters-in-law. Mamma trained me well.'

He'd always loved to cook, she remembered, especially if it was for herself. In fact, he'd always liked looking after her, being one of those rare men who was at his best if his wife was ill. The meal slipped down easily.

'What have you been doing since you went away?' he asked, pouring her a cup of tea. 'Did you return to the store?'

'Part time. I'm on maternity leave now, but they'll take me back later. While I wait I'm writing a book about the history of glass.'

'How are you managing with Venetian glass?' he asked wryly.

'Is there any other kind?' she riposted.

'You know my feelings about that. Can I help?'

'You could read my notes about Venetian glass and tell me what you think.'

'Fine, send them to me when—you get back.'

'I can do better,' she said, suddenly inspired. 'If I can use your computer I can break into mine.'

A few minutes' work brought her files up on Francesco's screen. He switched on his printer and the pages came flooding into the basket while she returned to her meal.

'All right?' he asked when she'd finished.

'Yes, it was delicious.'

'I think you should take a nap now. This is all a strain on you.'

His gentle tone was dangerous, she thought. It

reminded her of how lovely he could be to live with, making her forget things she'd be better off remembering.

'I should go back to the hotel,' she murmured.

'Please, Sonia, let me care for you and our child just a little.'

'All right. Thanks.'

He gave her his arm into the bedroom, settled her on the bed and went to close the shutters.

'No, leave them,' she begged. 'I like to look at the sky.'

He'd been right to make her rest, she thought, closing her eyes and feeling drowsiness overtake her. She thought she felt his lips pressed against her forehead before she slept.

When she awoke the light was fading, although it was still day. Sonia slid carefully off the bed and went to look out at the little *rio* below. The water was quiet and the paths alongside it were empty. Windows glowed in the gloom. The Venetians had hurried home to get on with their Christmas preparations, and now their doors were shut against the cold and all the warmth was within.

Looking along the *rio* to the left she saw where it met the Grand Canal. A water bus was just passing, sending little ripples along the narrow strip of water, making a small boat tied opposite bounce noisily in the water.

There had been a boat that first night, she remembered, a gondola tied up right beneath her hotel window. And whenever a vessel passed along the Grand Canal the waves had slapped against the gondola. At home her bedroom window was over a main road, and she cheerfully slept through trucks rumbling past. But in the quiet of Venice those light sounds had kept her awake.

Or perhaps it wasn't the sounds but the young man she'd met that day and known all her life, whose kiss had lived in her after he'd said goodnight. Long after his footsteps had faded along the flagstones, her whole body had been alive with the consciousness of him.

She stood now, listening to the silence of the flat, wondering if Francesco had gone out. She went quietly to the door and opened it. The main room was in a half light from one tiny lamp, and she almost didn't notice Francesco in the arm chair. As she crept across she saw that his head had fallen forward. His eyes were closed, he was breathing deeply and regularly.

There was a stool near the chair. Quietly she drew it forward and settled down beside him, looking up at his face.

With a pain she saw that the boyishness was gone for ever. There was a touch of hardness about the mobile mouth that had once been so merry. It had only been two and a half years since their marriage, but there were new lines on his face, and they weren't laughter lines. There was even a faint touch of grey at the sides.

But he's only thirty-six, she thought, dismayed. And hard on the heels of that thought came another, more painful.

I did this to him.

He had one arm on the side, the hand hanging free. Gently she took his hand between her own and studied it. Such a large, strong hand, such a gentle hand, that knew how to caress a woman for her delight. There was a small cut on one finger that looked as if it hadn't been attended to. He was always getting these little cuts, she remembered, because he involved himself so much in the process of glass-making. He loved to pick up half finished pieces and study them lovingly. And when he got home she would treat his cuts, and he would laugh and say, 'I'm indestructible. But don't stop. I love it when you look after me.'

Now she wondered how well or how often she'd looked after him.

She was struck by the bareness of the apartment, so close to Christmas. Where were the decorations? Francesco had put up tinsel and holly as soon as possible—'like a big kid,' she'd teased him, the first year. But the second year, their last Christmas together, the joke had sounded hollow as their marriage disintegrated, and the pretty lights shone down on emptiness.

And now this—this nothing at all.

The flat was spotless. He was good at house-work, and doubtless Giovanna had enjoyed helping out. But 'looking after' was something else. Suddenly her heart ached as she thought of him re-turning to this lonely flat and that smiling picture, with nobody to make a fuss about a tiny cut. Instinctively she placed her cheek against the back of his hand and rubbed it gently. The remembered feel of it sent a pain through her. How often, how gently these hands had held her. And how empty life was without him.

A slight sound made her look up to find him watching her sadly.

'I've missed you,' he said.

'I've missed you too.'

'I thought I'd never see you here again.'

'Please, darling, it doesn't mean anything. I love you but I can't live with you. I can't fit into your world and you could never be happy away from here. At the start it all looked so easy that we didn't look at practical things, but we have to look at them now.'

He touched her bulge. 'Isn't this a practical thing?'

It would be so easy to say, 'I want to stay here and never leave you again. I love you and we'll work it out somehow.' So easy. And so impossible.

Like someone who'd suddenly found herself tottering on the edge of a precipice, she drew back with a sharp breath, looking for a distraction.

She found one in the printed sheets that had fallen out of his hand onto the floor. They bore scribbled marks as though he'd read them intently.

'What did you think of my writing?' she asked hastily. 'I expect it read like nonsense to you.'

'No,' he rubbed his eyes as though forcing himself back to reality. 'I've made a few notes that may help you, but you've done an excellent job.' He added wryly, 'You really do understand Venetian glass now.'

Was there any conversation that didn't turn into a minefield? He was saying that Venetian glass was all she understood. The people were still a mystery to her.

He read her thoughts and added quickly, 'No, Sonia, please, I didn't mean—'

'It's all right. Whatever you meant to say, it's the truth, and we both know it.' She rose to her feet. 'Take a walk with me.'

'A walk? Where?'

'To the Garibaldi Gardens. I want to see what they look like now.'

'Cold and damp, like everywhere else,' he said, also getting to his feet. 'Is that why you want to go?'

It was true she wanted to see the place at its worst, in the hope of dispelling other memories. She'd forgotten his flashes of insight, how unexpectedly shrewd he could be at reading her sometimes, and how dense at others.

They made their way along the grey waterfront, the lagoon hidden by the dense mist that shrouded it.

'Do you really remember that day?' Francesco asked.

'Oh yes,' she said sadly. 'I've never forgotten it.'

'You remember how I proposed to you?'

'You never did exactly propose to me,' she recalled wryly. 'You just informed the whole of Venice that we were engaged, then you promised me nobody would take it seriously, and left me to find out that everyone was planning the wedding. Your sisters-in-law had chosen our curtains before I even met them.'

'That's how it's done in Venice,' he reminded her.

'I know.'

Silence. It had been an unfortunate remark, reminding her of all she couldn't come to terms with.

'I was afraid to ask you direct,' Francesco said. 'It happened so fast for me and I couldn't believe it was the same for you. So I sort of built a wall around you first.' He made a face. 'But you can't build walls around people. They always escape.'

In the quiet their footsteps echoed on the gleaming flagstones, and their silhouettes approached in a small puddle, then faded again.

'This place is full of ghosts,' she murmured. Then she wished the words unsaid, for lost love was a kind of ghost, whispering around corners, reminding them of things best forgotten. But it was magical just the same, not the glorious magic of summer, but the unearthly magic of soft lights and memories.

A few minutes walk brought them to the garden. Sonia was picturing the stone benches that stood at intervals against the railings, overhung with trees. 'Their' bench had been the second one down on the left. It would be visible almost as soon as they entered, and suddenly she didn't want to look. There had been so much joy here, and now it was all over. As they went through the gates she found herself averting her gaze. When she could do so no longer she braced herself and looked at the bench.

It wasn't there.

'This isn't the place,' she said. 'It must be further along.'

'No, it was the second one down,' Francesco said. 'That's where it was, where those two stones are sticking out of the ground.'

'But it's *gone*,' she whispered, feeling the chill wind cut through her.

'I'm afraid so. I'm sorry, I didn't know. It was here a couple of weeks ago.'

'But it can't be gone,' she cried desperately. 'It was *ours*.'

The bench had gone, just like the sentimental illusions it represented. This should have been her moment of vindication. Instead she felt the anguish rise up to swamp her, and the next moment she was sobbing with heartbreak.

'Darling,' Francesco said, taking her in his arms. 'Please—it's only a bench.'

'It isn't,' she wept. 'It's everything—the end of everything—don't you see? It's all over—everything we had.'

'I thought that was over long ago,' he said gently.

'It was, but—now it really is,' she choked, grief stricken. Logic and common sense couldn't help her now. Everything had gone and now there was nothing but emptiness. All her defences seemed to collapse at the same moment, and she sobbed bitterly in Francesco's arms.

'We had so much,' she wept. 'Where did it go?'

'It hasn't gone,' he said urgently. 'It's still there. We don't have to let it go.'

She shook her head stubbornly. 'No more illusions,' she said.

'Illusions?' he said angrily. 'You thought if we came here in winter you'd prove that our love was no more than a summer illusion. Well? Have you proved it?'

Dumbly she looked at him, her face still wet. He relented, touching her cheek with gentle fingers. 'I didn't mean to shout at you. Come back home and we'll talk some more.'

But she shook her head. 'I'm going back to the hotel. I have to pack. I'm going tomorrow.'

'No, not yet. It's too soon.'

She took his face between her hands. 'Darling, darling Francesco, listen to me. It was my fault it went wrong. I've known that for ages. I'd never had a family, and then yours was so—so much.'

'I know about "so much",' he agreed. 'But there's "so much" and "so much". So much interference, so much nosiness, so much friendship, so much love.'

'I guess I just couldn't cope with the closeness. It suffocated me. I don't know what families do—I never did.'

'So what's your answer? Go and live like a hermit, and teach our child to be as isolated as yourself?'

'You're saying I don't know how to take love. And maybe you're right.'

'Then learn. There's still time. Take the love we've all tried to give you.'

'You make it sound so easy, but you know it isn't. It wouldn't work. I can't change. We'd soon be quarrelling again.'

'You're a stubborn woman,' he said bitterly. 'You're leaving me for no better reason than that you said you would. Can't you admit that you were wrong?'

'It seems that I can't,' she said sadly. 'I never could, could I? That's how I made you so unhappy.'

'You made me unhappy on the day you left,' he said. 'Never at any other time.'

'Oh, darling, that's not true. You know how often I made you angry—'

'Angry isn't unhappy. Anger doesn't destroy a marriage when people love each other. It doesn't have to destroy us. And how can you travel now? The baby—'

'The baby isn't due for another three weeks.'

'Do you know how close to Christmas it is?'

'That's why I must hurry. If I leave tomorrow I have just time to get home before Christmas Eve.'

'And you'll return alone to an empty flat, with nobody there if anything happens. And you prefer that to staying here with your family, with a man who loves you. *Thank you.*'

But his heart sank as he spoke. Looking into her face he saw sadness but no yielding.

'I'll take you to the hotel,' he said with a sigh.

At the hotel he insisted on coming as far as her room, and seeing her settled onto the bed.

'You're tired,' he said. 'I shouldn't have let you walk so far.'

'I'm all right, really. I'll go to bed as soon as I've eaten something. Would you call the station for me and see if there's a train about noon tomorrow?'

He did so, and made her a reservation.

'I'll call for you tomorrow and take you to the station,' he said.

'If you're sure you want to—'

He swore. 'No, I don't *want* to,' he said bitterly. 'You know what I want. But I'll be damned if I let you drag your luggage there alone. I'll be here at ten thirty.'

As he strode away from the hotel the wet flagstones gleamed under the lights, and his footsteps echoed mournfully. He found he was walking slower and slower, as though his feet knew that his heart didn't want to return to the empty apartment where there had once been so much love, and where now there was nothing.

He let his feet follow their own instincts, and they took him to the little chapel of St Michele, as he had known they would. There was nobody there, and when he had lit a candle he sat down wearily and looked up to the plump little Madonna with her friendly face and giggling baby. He thought of his own baby, whose laughter he wouldn't hear, and closed his eyes.

'If I still believed in miracles I'd ask for one more—just a little one—'

At last he opened his eyes. All was silence in the little chapel. Looking up he saw that the Madonna was looking a little shabby. After all, she was only wood. Suddenly he felt foolish.

Reluctantly he got to his feet, wondering what had come over him. He was a grown man now, and the age of miracles was past.

CHAPTER SIX

AT THE hotel Sonia called Room Service and had supper sent up. She had little appetite but knew she must keep her strength up for the journey to come. When she'd eaten as much as she could she sat by the window, trying to find the energy to undress and go to bed.

But it wasn't bodily weariness that troubled her, so much as a restlessness of spirit. There was something left undone, and she, a neat and orderly person, must tie up the ends before she left Venice forever. Resolutely she rose, put on her coat, and walked out of the hotel. Snow was beginning to fall, obscuring her vision, but by now she knew the streets of Venice like a Venetian, and she made her way easily to the Hospital of San Domenica.

'I'm Signora Bartini's daughter-in-law,' she explained to the nurse on duty. 'May I sit with her for a while?'

'She's asleep—' the nurse said cautiously.

'I won't disturb her.'

Giovanna was lying with her eyes closed and her face seemed more shrunken than ever. Sonia went to sit quietly beside the bed and took one of the old woman's thin hands in hers. At once Giovanna's fingers tightened on hers, and she stirred, but didn't awaken. Sonia grew still, and the two women stayed like that, motionless, for a long time.

After a while the nurse slipped in with a cup of tea.

'Excuse me, *signorina*,' she said, 'but may I ask your first name?'

'Sonia.'

'Oh,' she seemed disappointed. 'I thought perhaps you were Maria.'

Sonia was suddenly alert. 'Why do you ask that?'

'Sometimes she's confused and she talks a lot about Maria, but it's hard to tell which one she means.'

'Which one?'

'Sometimes it's clear she's talking about her daughter, the one who died as a baby. She showed me the picture once. After fifty years she still remembers her as though it was yesterday. But of course you know all about that. She also seems convinced that she has a daughter-in-law called Maria, who will come and visit her. But I think they've all come now, and none of them are called Maria.'

She bustled out, leaving Sonia feeling as though she'd been through a wringer. Doors had flown open in her mind at once, and behind them were a dozen pictures, never understood before, but so tragically clear now.

Fifty years ago Giovanna's first baby had died at birth. Afterwards she'd had so many children that it had occurred to nobody that her heart still grieved for her long-ago firstborn. And how could she have told anyone how she still suffered, that proud, un-yielding woman who found it so hard to admit that she loved people and needed them?

Like me?

Sonia quickly pushed the thought away, but she knew that in her own awkward way her mother-in-law had tried to reach out to her. The words, 'But of course, you know all about that,' uttered in inno-cence, were like a reproach. Giovanna had managed to tell this stranger, but not the daughter-in-law she would have liked to tell.

If I'd been gentler she might have found a way to confide in me, Sonia thought sadly. I was the one she chose.

The nurse had mentioned a picture. Quietly Sonia pulled open the drawer and lifted out the picture she found there. It was black and white and a little faded, but she could still clearly see the young woman cradling her first baby, her face alight with pride and joy. Tears stung Sonia's eyes at how soon that joy was to be extinguished.

She sighed, seeing the pictures of her married life float past, all changed under the differently coloured light that had suddenly been turned on them. Giovanna's visits that she interpreted as criticism— were they that, or a way of reaching out from a woman who didn't know how to use words? Her 'interference' with the housework could have been no more than her clumsy way of helping Sonia study; the name Maria from a woman who could still be hurt by it.

And when Francesco had asked her about it Giovanna had denied it, because she couldn't bear to explain. It was all so simple if you had the key.

The door opened quietly behind her and Tomaso slipped into the room.

'*Grazie,*' he said softly when he saw Sonia. 'I knew you would come back.'

'*Poppa*, I didn't know myself until half an hour ago.'

'But I knew,' he patted her hand, 'because I know your kind heart.'

His way of always thinking the best of her made her feel awkward. 'I wasn't very kind,' she murmured. 'Otherwise I'd have known about this.' She showed him the picture. 'Why did nobody ever tell me?'

'Because she would never have it mentioned,' Tomaso said sadly. 'On the day our daughter died she put all her baby clothes away and made me promise never to speak of it. I thought her heart would ease when our next child was born, but it never did. Our sons know nothing. It's as though it didn't happen.'

'Did you want to deal with it that way?' she asked curiously.

He gave a shrug that had something forlorn about it. 'In those days—men were not supposed to—I don't think it ever occurred to her that I was unhappy, too.'

'No,' she said softly. 'We do a lot of harm in our way.'

'We?'

'Women like Giovanna and me.'

'Ah, you see it. I wondered if you did.'

'Poppa, what does *"No esser come mi,"* mean?'

'It means "Don't be like me". Why?'

'It's what she said when I came here earlier. She was trying to warn me. Yes, I see it, but I can't change it, *Poppa*. It would take a miracle to do that, and I don't believe in them.'

'Not even at Christmas?' he asked sadly.

'Not even at Christmas.'

She looked kindly at her mother-in-law, her face still frowning in her sleep. Nowadays, she thought, there would be counselling and support groups. But fifty years ago, the young Giovanna Bartini had coped with her grief by denying it. And the denial had tortured her for years, until another Maria had arrived, offering a kind of hope, which, in turn had been destroyed. Sonia's heart ached for her, and ached even more because she knew it was too late to help her now.

She replaced the picture and kissed the sleeping woman.

'Goodbye, Mamma,' she whispered. 'I'm sorry I couldn't be what you wanted. I don't know how any more. But I did come to see you—as you always knew I would.'

On her way out she noticed the Madonna standing in her little niche by the door. This was the one Mother Lucia had said was good at solving problems. Unlike Francesco's jolly peasant Madonna, she was coolly beautiful and aloof, but her arm about her baby was secure and possessive.

'It's easy to talk,' Sonia told her silently. 'But, like I told him, I see it but I can't change it. I'm trapped inside myself and there's no way out. No miracles. Not for Giovanna, not for me.'

Then, in an unexpected flash of rebellion, she added, 'I'll bet *his* Madonna would find a miracle for him.'

Francesco was at her hotel promptly next morning. She was already down in reception, and he carried her bags out to the landing stage where the motor boat was waiting for them. He got in and reached up for her, putting his arms around her bulky body, feeling her cling to him against the boat's sway.

'Are you all right?' he asked softly, and saw her strained smile. He wondered why he'd asked. How could either of them ever be all right again?

For the short journey along the Grand Canal he sat with her hand in his, until at last the broad steps of the station came into view. The sight shocked him with its reminder of how little time was left.

He carried her bag onto the train, saw her to her seat and sat beside her.

'We're in good time,' she said, smiling.

'Yes,' he agreed in a forced tone. 'Another ten minutes.'

Sonia wished she could find something to say. In ten minutes the train would carry her away from him forever. She couldn't stop it happening. But would she if she could? She no longer knew that, or anything except that the pain over her heart was intolerable. To cover it she said something about Italian trains always being on time and he smiled and nodded.

Silence. The seconds ticked past. But words were easy. It was the living up to them was hard, and the sense of failure crushed her.

'Well, perhaps you'd better go,' she said. 'You don't want to be caught here when it moves.'

'Sonia—'

'No,' she cried desperately. 'I can't.'

'You can. All it takes is two words. "I'll stay." Say them. *Say them.*'

'Words are easy. Remember those wonderful vows we exchanged? But they were just words in the end. If I stayed it would end the same way.'

He stroked her face. There was nothing more to say.

Doors were slamming, people moving quickly. It was time.

'Goodbye,' he said softly. 'Goodbye, my—' The words ended in a choke and he pressed his lips against her hands. 'Goodbye, goodbye.'

'Darling,' she whispered, *'please—'*

She didn't even know what she was asking for. Please, let me go. Please let something happen to stop me going. But the pain was getting worse.

'It's all right,' he said. 'I won't make it hard for you. Goodbye.'

He rose to leave. She rose with him. And suddenly the pain wasn't just in her heart but everywhere, stabbing her violently so that she gasped and clung to him.

'What is it?' he demanded sharply.

'Nothing, I just—*ah! The baby*—' The pain came again and she clutched her stomach.

'*Mio dio!* I have to get you to a hospital.'

'Yes—please,' she gasped. 'Quickly.'

With one arm firmly about Sonia he helped her off the train and guided her to a bench, leaving her sitting there while he dashed back for her bag. He just made it back onto the platform before the train began to move.

'Francesco—' She reached out a hand to him.

'I'm here,' he said, swiftly coming to her.

'Don't leave me.'

'Never. Hold onto me, *amor mia*, and we'll soon be at the hospital.'

Station staff had seen what was happening and were rushing to help them. A man ran up with a wheelchair and Francesco assisted her into it.

'Quickly,' she said.

'I'll have you at the hospital in no time,' he said tensely.

The word had gone around and people stepped aside to let them through. Someone hailed a motor boat, and by the time they were out of the station at the top of the steps it was waiting below. A crowd was gathering, understanding what was happening, and full of cheerful good nature. Some men rushed forward to help steady the wheelchair as Francesco eased it down the steps. Friendly arms stretched out to help her into the boat. The air was filled with shouts of encouragement.

'*Grazie, grazie!*' Francesco called back.

She'd forgotten about these people, Sonia thought: how kind they were, how they loved life and welcomed a birth. It was as though everyone in Venice was part of her family, welcoming, happy for her. As they chugged away a smiling woman called something.

'What did she say?' Sonia asked.

'She said it's nice to have a Christmas baby,' Francesco translated.

'Oh, yes,' she murmured. 'It's Christmas—isn't it? The day after tomorrow—or maybe the day after that—I forget?'

'Don't worry about anything,' Francesco said gently. 'Just think about the baby.'

She gasped against the pain and gripped him tightly. Suddenly there were no more words, no more misery or anger, just Francesco and the comfort of his arms about her, the sense of safety she found in burrowing against him. The boat bucked and she held him tighter.

'Is it much further?' she moaned.

'We're going to the same hospital Mamma's in. Not much further. Look at me, darling.'

His voice seemed to hypnotise her into doing what he said. Looking up, she found his eyes fixed on her, holding hers as though demanding that she forget everything but him. And suddenly the easiest thing was to follow his lead and let him take care of her.

'Trust me,' he whispered, 'everything's going to be all right.'

'Don't let go of me,' she begged.

She hardly knew what she said, but when he replied, 'Never in life,' it was just what she wanted to hear, and she relaxed.

The driver called ahead to alert the hospital and they arrived to find a team awaiting them. As they began to hurry her away Sonia gripped Francesco's hand. 'Come with me,' she insisted.

The nurse looked uncertain. 'Well—'

'I want him with me.'

'I'm staying,' Francesco said firmly.

Sonia drew a sharp breath of pain and after that there was no more argument. Francesco helped her onto the trolley and then they were on their way to the delivery room. The world became a ceiling sliding past overhead. Somewhere, walking close was Francesco, but she couldn't see him. She reached out a frantic hand and felt it gripped in his strong one.

'I'm here,' he promised.

'Darling—do something for me.'

'Anything.'

'Go and tell your mother about this.'

'Of course I will—in a while. I don't want to leave you now.'

'Yes, yes, she must know at once. And then call all the others.'

He frowned. 'Won't later do?'

'No, they'll want to share the excitement while it's happening, not find out when it's all over.'

He leaned close to her. 'Don't you want to keep this for just us?'

She smiled. 'It *is* just for us. We won't lose that because we share it. Hurry now and go to your mother. Tell her—tell her Maria came back. She'll understand.'

Something in her voice alerted him. After studying her face for a moment he nodded and said, 'I'm going.'

He slipped away, and for the next few minutes the medical staff worked to prepare her for her labour. Mother Lucia appeared, smiling broadly. 'Looks like you're going to win your bet,' Sonia murmured.

'Oh, I knew I would.'

Francesco returned, wearing a hospital gown. 'Mamma's thrilled,' he said. 'It's transformed her.'

'Did you give her my message?'

'Yes, and she sent you her love.'

Sonia's reply was lost in a gasp of pain. She reached for his hand again and gripped it tightly.

'Maybe it won't be too long,' he said, looking hopefully at Mother Lucia.

The little nun looked doubtful. 'First baby?'

'Yes,' Sonia said.

'They usually take a bit longer.'

As she'd said, it didn't happen fast, and even with the help of gas and air the birth wasn't easy. Sonia braced herself against the pain, telling herself that she was strong and had endured a good deal, on her own. But Francesco, the charming, spoilt child of the family, raised to be light-hearted and talk his way out of trouble: what had he ever endured?

Then she saw the wretchedness of the last few months in his eyes, and knew the answer.

'I have no right to give up on us so easily,' she murmured. 'You don't hate me?'

He leaned close, and whispered. 'I'll be honest, *amor mia*, I hated you at the start. No woman had

ever left me before, and the one who did was the
only one who mattered. I told myself that you would
return. I believed it for months before I faced the fact
that you were as stubborn as I.'

'Too stubborn,' she said. 'I should have come
back long ago, but—'

'I know, I know. We'll learn together. We'll have
help now.'

She winced as another pain came. He mopped
her brow and they fell silent, content simply to be
together with no more need for words. Everything
in the world was concentrated here, her hand in her
husband's as the two of them fought to bring this
new life into the world, a life that their love had
created. She fixed her eyes on him, and saw that his
own eyes were full of anguish for her suffering.

'Darling,' he said desperately.

'I'm—all right—' she gasped. 'This is normal.'
'Amor di dio!'

The pain tightened its grip but she pushed the
thought aside. She must make him feel better.
'Don't worry,' she murmured. 'We're going to have
a beautiful baby.'

'Any minute now,' Mother Lucia said trium-
phantly. 'One more push.'

And it was all over.

'It's a boy,' Francesco said in a voice she'd never
heard him use before.

The cry grew louder, stronger, until it was a

mighty bellow. Over the baby's head the parents' eyes met in mutual pride. This one was going to tell the world when he grew up.

At last her son was in her arms, unbelievably tiny, but vigorous and perfect. And the feeling sweeping over her was like nothing she'd ever known before. This was love, not the sweet romance that would fade, but an intense, primitive emotion that shook her until she was no longer the same person, but a new one, who'd discovered what was important and would do anything to protect it.

Francesco too was watching the child, transfixed, so that she was able to study his face, unnoticed. She saw again the change that she'd first noticed in the flat. He was older, a little weary with sad experience, but now full of a profound joy.

The fierce love that streamed from her to enfold her child seemed to have no end. It flowed on, encompassing the man also, and after him the whole world. But him above all.

'Francesco…' she whispered. 'Are you still there?'

'*Si, amor mia,*' he said, understanding her at once. 'I am still here. I always will be.'

'You were far away,' she murmured.

'So were you. I didn't know how to find you. But now that I have, I shall never let you go again. Either of you.'

'Mmm,' she murmured sleepily. The long hours of hard work were catching up with her. She felt the soft touch of his lips on her forehead, and the movement as he eased the baby out of her arms.

'Go to sleep now,' he told her. 'You can leave our son with me. He will be quite safe.'

Of course he would, because here was safety, life, love, all the things she'd missed since the day she'd left them for reasons she could no longer remember.

That was her last thought as she drifted into sleep.

When she awoke it was dark outside the windows, and she was full of blissful contentment. By her bed stood a cot, holding her sweetly sleeping child. For a moment she gazed on him in awe, but then her eyes searched the room anxiously until they found what she needed to see—Francesco, dozing in an armchair by the window. She relaxed. He was here. All was well.

An instinct seemed to alert him, and he awoke immediately, coming over to the bed, smiling. She opened her arms and he came into them, holding her tightly as never before.

'I love you,' he said. 'I love you more now than ever before.'

'How could I ever have gone away from you?' she asked, 'Loving you as I do.'

'Tell me that you love me,' he begged. 'Let me hear you say it.'

'I love you. I don't know how I could ever have thought I didn't—or that I could kill my feelings. How could I have tried to take your baby away from you? How could I leave you?'

'Swear that you'll never leave me again.'

'I'll never even think of it. I couldn't bear to be apart from you.' Something occurred to her. 'While I was asleep I understood the magic.'

'You understood?' he asked cautiously.

'Winter or summer, the magic was still there—because you were there. It wasn't a holiday romance at all.'

'I always knew that.'

'And tried to make me see it. Now I do.'

'I went to see Mamma after you went to sleep. She's longing to come and see you, and her new grandson.'

'Can she get out of bed?'

'She perked up wonderfully when she heard the news. Can I fetch her?'

'Yes, of course.'

When he'd gone she went to the cradle and lifted her child. She felt well and strong for the first time in months. There was an armchair by the window and she went to sit there, looking out at the darkness and the lights over the Grand Canal.

The feel of the baby against her was unutterably sweet. And now she knew how Giovanna had felt. To lose this precious scrap would break her heart, and it would stay broken, no matter how many other children were born afterwards.

'Such a family I've given you,' she murmured against the child's head. 'There's Ruggiero and Giuseppe, and Benito and Enrico, and Wenda and Soo, and all your cousins. You'll never come to any harm, because there'll always be one of them looking out for you at the corner of the street. And if you should ever wander away in the wrong direction, the whole "United Nations" will get together to bring you safely home again. That's what families are for.'

Francesco appeared with Giovanna in a wheel-chair, Tomaso walking behind. The old woman's joy transformed her, and for the first time she turned to Sonia a truly heartfelt smile.

'Come and meet your newest grandchild,' Sonia said.

Francesco wheeled his mother across the floor until she was close to Sonia, who leaned forward to give her a good view of the child. Giovanna looked long into the baby's crumpled face, then raised her eyes to her daughter-in-law.

'Thank you—Maria,' she said softly.

And now she didn't mind the name, because she understood everything Giovanna had been too proud to tell her. Besides, to be called Mary at Christmas was a compliment.

'You were right,' she said to Giovanna, 'it changes everything.'

She spoke in a low voice, to include only the two of them. Francesco looked from one to the other, not having heard, but sensing somehow that all was well.

From beyond the window came the sounds of revelry.

'It's the Christmas Eve procession,' Francesco said.

Still holding the baby Sonia went to stand in the window to watch the torchlit gondolas gliding down the canal. Behind her, Francesco put his arms around her, enfolding her and their baby. She could see the three of them reflected in the dark window.

The reflection also showed her the moment when Ruggiero appeared in the doorway, with Wenda, Giuseppe and Lin Soo, their children, then another brother, another wife, a nephew, uncle, aunt, until the whole vast mob of the Bartini family was there, stretching out into the corridor, all eager to see the newest addition, but waiting for her signal.

'Invite them in,' she said to Francesco.

He beckoned to his family. Smiling, she watched them in the window's reflection, as they came in, one by one, until they filled the room as far as she could see, their faces beaming with joy at this birth, and rebirth. It had taken too long, but she had finally come home.

It was as though all the world was there. And at its heart, a man, a woman, and a newborn child.

There are 24 timeless classics in the Mills & Boon® 100th Birthday Collection

Two of these beautiful stories are out each month. Make sure you collect them all!

If you have missed any of these books, log on to www.millsandboon.co.uk to order your copies online.